MW01130736

The Iceman always comes on Tuesday

a novel

JAMES MASSE

Based on a screenplay by Vito Rocco Perrotti

DISCLAIMER

The Iceman always comes on Tuesday is a work of fiction. The names, characters, places and events are all products of the creator's imaginations, or have been used in a fictitious manner and are not to be misconstrued as real. Any resemblance to persons, living or dead, is entirely coincidental.

All rights are reserved. No part of this novel may be used or reproduced in any manner whatsoever without written permission from the author.

Every effort has been made to provide a quality reading experience, however, writers, editors, and even technology are all imperfect. Please report any typos or formatting issues to AuthorJamesMasse@yahoo.com

Copyright © 2020 James Masse

All rights reserved.

ISBN: 9781096099727

CONTENTS

Chapter One

Strong hands at the reins

The summer of 1947 was hot, humid, and beautifully polluted. Smog from factories and automobiles hovered over postwar Chicago like a plague. The sun was somewhere up there, too, trying its damnedest to shine down while being suffocated with the byproduct of late forties prosperity in America. Downtown Chicago was always busy, but on this particular morning Michigan Avenue was a whole new ball game. It was a battlefield of Studebakers, Pierce Arrows and Model-T's honking and swerving all over the street.

The culprit for the early morning madness was an iceman in a horse-drawn carriage. Stacio Jasinski was a hard fella in his early forties. A hard chin, hard head, hard body, and two hard, calloused hands made up the hardest working man in Illinois. His powerful fists gripped the reins of his painfully slow horse, who was still well-groomed and beautiful for her age. Stacio and his mare should have been painted in black and white while everything around them was in

1

color. They were so out of place, so unwilling and unable to conform. He and his horse, his carriage, and the ice business were all stuck, frozen in time while the modern world passed them by.

'Degan's Icehouse' was barely visible on the sides of the tattered canvas that covered the carriage's old wooden skeleton. Stacio lifted the reins and brought his old girl to a halt. He was so calm and patient, just waving at the crazed drivers to go around him. The cars honked and yelled as they swerved by, but Stacio just smiled, tipped his cap and proceeded to do his job.

He climbed out of his carriage, fixed his white tank top and adjusted his suspenders. His arms and shoulders were extremely defined, ice was a heavy job. He tucked his brown hair into his gray flat cap and brushed his hand over his horse's mane. "How are you, Chestnut?" he asked. "Last stop and we head home, girl." He looked into his horse's eyes when he spoke to her.

He wasn't a wealthy man so he took good care of everything he had, and by the way he pet this old horse you could tell he cared for her dearly. She wasn't just a means of transporting his ice, she was one of his oldest friends.

Stacio had few friends and even fewer enemies. Most of his life his only true nemesis was the sun, which was the case for most icemen, and the reason he always started his route in darkness. However, it wouldn't be long before Stacio found himself standing toe-to-toe with two brand new enemies, but we'll get into that later.

He looked up at the building, lifting his hand to his brow to shade his eyes. This was his last customer of the day, but the 'Need Ice' sign wasn't in her window like it was every other Tuesday morning.

"She must have forgotten," he mumbled to his horse. "What do you say, Chestnut?"

Stacio was a man of few words, he talked to his horse just as much as he talked to anyone else. He smiled and patted her rump as he walked by. "You're a good girl," he said.

His piercing blue eyes scanned the street as he made his way to the back of the carriage. More cars flew by, honking and yelling, but he just shrugged his shoulders and kept on working. Stacio was a hard-headed, determined man, he'd been like that since he was a boy. Unless one of the cars ran him down where he stood, nothing could've stopped him from doing what he set out to do. He was an iceman, and he would deliver his ice.

3

Stacio was peaceful and content with his mundane routine, it was honest work that put food on his family's table. He dropped his tailgate and brushed off a large block of ice before dragging it out to the ledge.

"Iceman. Iceman," three children yelled, storming around the side of his carriage with empty cups in their hands. "Ice. Please, Stash, it's so hot out here," one of the kids begged.

Stacio turned away from them and reached deeper into the carriage to grab an ice pick. He turned to the children, growling and posing like a monster. "Rah!" Stacio and the three boys laughed, and then he used the ice pick to chip ice into each of their cups.

"Thanks a lot, Stash," two of the boys yelled, running off.

Stacio tossed the ice pick back into the carriage and ruffled the last boy's hair. "Stay out of trouble," he said, "and stay out of the street."

"We will," said the boy, nodding his head as he ran off. "Thanks again for the ice."

Stacio reached back into the carriage and grabbed a pair of metal tongs, gripping them around the seventy-five pound block of ice. He took a deep breath, lifting it out of the carriage and shuffling toward the old tenement building.

Stacio's whole body flexed, looking like a chiseled, granite statue as he labored up seven stories with that small glacier. Most of the flights were barely lit and some were pitch black, but he just kept on climbing. When he finally reached the top floor, a small boy opened the door and said, "Hey, Stash, come on in."

"Thank you, Billy."

"You're welcome. Mom's inside," he said, pointing over his shoulder.

Stacio took a step into the house as Francis emerged from the kitchen. She was a very attractive, middle-aged, apron-wearing housewife. She was happy to see him at first, but a frown spread across her face when she noticed the ice. "Oh, Stash, I'm afraid we don't need ice today," she said. "The sign… it's not in the window."

"But today's Tuesday," said Stacio, resting the ice on the top of his boot. "I thought maybe you forgot the sign. I didn't want Billy's milk to spoil."

"Yeah, mom, today is Tuesday," said Billy. "The Iceman always comes on Tuesday."

Stacio turned to face Billy, he smiled at him and said, "The boy's right." His smile faded when he turned back to Francis and noticed how emotional she'd become. "Is everything all right?" he asked.

She dabbed her eyes with the bottom of her apron and said, "Yes, it's just that…" She took a deep breath and stepped to the side, revealing her brand new electric refrigerator. "I'm so sorry, Stash, it was a surprise from my husband. If I had known I would've told you right away. I feel terrible."

Stacio just stood there, speechless and covered in sweat. He forced a smile and nodded, but the defeat on his face revealed the sting of another lost customer. Remember when I mentioned Stacio finding himself two new enemies? One of them was the electric refrigerator. It was cleaner, easier, and a whole lot more convenient than the old block of ice. A great new appliance for anyone who could afford it, but not good at all for Stacio and his livelihood.

Sooner or later, everyone in Chicago would have a fancy new refrigerator. Everyone except the Jasinski family, of course. Even if Stacio could afford it he would never want one. Machines had too many moving parts that needed fixing all the time. Ice was simple, it was reliable and it always did its job. Ice made sense to Stacio.

Being an iceman was all Stacio knew. The thought of a world

with no iceman didn't seem like a world he wanted to be part of. It was gonna be an uphill battle, maybe an impossible fight to win, but he wasn't gonna quit. He would never quit the ice business or anything else he set his mind to.

"Francis, you were my very first customer," he said.

"I know. I'm sorry. I feel so terrible, I had no idea that he was-"

Stacio cut her off, but in a polite way, "No need to explain, I understand. I just want to say thank you for many years," he said, lugging the block of ice back toward the door. Billy opened the door for him and ran out of the room.

"Here, you should have this," said Francis, pulling a few coins from her apron.

"You want the ice?" he asked.

"No, I just-"

"No money then. Thank you," he said, stepping out the door. "Goodbye, Billy," he hollered back into the house.

"Wait," said Billy, running toward the door with a carrot in his hand. "Give this to Chestnut and tell her it's from me."

"Will do," said Stacio, balancing the ice with one hand while sliding the carrot into his pocket with the other.

7

"Thanks a lot," said Billy.

Stacio smiled, he nodded to Billy and then to Francis, struggling to get the block of ice down the first few steps. The door closed behind him and he let out a long sigh. *Lost another one.*

"Wait," said Francis, opening the door and stepping out, "I have fresh muffins. They're your favorite, you must take some."

She placed a rolled up towel on top of the block of ice. Stacio smiled.

"I'm sorry, again," she said.

"No worries. Thank you for the muffins."

"You're very welcome, Stacio," she stuttered, struggling to hold back tears.

"Good day, Francis."

Stacio tipped his cap and continued his grueling climb down the dark stairwell. When he finally got to the street his entire body ached. He heaved the ice back into the carriage and slammed the tailgate shut. He stretched his sore back, grabbed his muffins and walked to the front of the carriage. He set the muffins down on his seat and took the carrot from his pocket.

"Losing this one hurts more than all the others," he said, feeding

Chestnut the bent carrot. She took the whole thing in two bites. "You worked hard today, let's get you home."

Stacio climbed into the carriage and grabbed the reins. Before he pulled away, a horse mounted police officer rode up next to him and stopped. "I saw you toss the ice back in," the cop said. "Another Frigidaire, huh?"

Stacio shrugged his shoulders.

"I guess it's a bad time to ask when you plan on switching to a truck," the officer said. "You got Michigan Avenue upside down again."

"I prefer my horse," said Stacio. "You're on a horse."

"Yeah, but once the city puts me in an automobile, I'll never have a sore ass again," he laughed.

Stacio smiled.

"Stash, come on," he said. "How many citations do I gotta give you before your thick Polak head understands?"

"I'm afraid the fines are much cheaper than a new truck."

"Yeah, Yeah, Yeah. I'm gonna let you go today, but keep that old hag off Michigan Avenue. Please, before one of these lunatics clobbers the both of you."

"Thank you," said Stacio, unraveling the towel and offering him a muffin.

The cop grabbed a muffin and tipped his cap. "Thanks, Stash, have yourself a good day."

Stacio nodded at the cop and took a bite of his own muffin before continuing down Michigan Avenue.

Chapter Two

The last holdout

Stacio and his family were the proud owners of the only working farm left on the outskirts of Chicago. It was the last holdout, but it was alive and well. During the postwar construction boom developers bought out the rest of the farms and built small houses anywhere they could squeeze them. The once beautiful land around the farm had been ravaged by suburban sprawl, but thanks to Grandpa, who shoved a shotgun in the face of anyone brave enough to knock on his door, the Jasinski farm was still standing.

Stacio's youngest son, Michael, sat on the steps with a harmonica pressed to his lips. He was only ten, but he played with the soul of an old New Orleans native. The house was green with a beige wraparound porch, both colors weathered and faded. Though everything about it was still beautiful, time hadn't been kind to this once proud property. A barn sat on the front side of the home, an impressive structure with the same olive clapboard as the house. Like two lizards ready to shed their skin, both buildings were in desperate need of restoration.

Stacio's other two boys; Stevie, twelve, and Stanley, fourteen, were playing baseball in the front yard. Stevie pitched to Stanley. The strike zone was painted on a huge maple tree behind home plate. The pitcher's mound was a patch of dirt and all four bases were lids from old bushels.

Stacio waved to his boys as he came down the driveway. All three boys waved back, but Michael lit up like a Christmas tree. Michael always lit up when he saw his father. Stacio loved all three of his boys unconditionally, and even though he'd never admit it or say it out loud, he loved Michael the most. They were very close, so close that Michael was probably Stacio's other best friend, second only to Chestnut.

Stacio pulled into the barn and opened a small leather pouch to count his meager earnings. He moved coins around with his finger, shaking his head and snapping the pouch shut. *Tomorrow will be better,* he thought, looking up and waving as Michael came running into the barn.

"Papa. Papa."

Stacio smiled and hopped out of the carriage. "You know what to do," he said, giving Michael a quick hug before handing him a pail.

Michael lifted the lid from a large barrel of oats and filled the pail.

"Only half a pail, Michael."

"But, Papa, I always fill it."

"Only half a pail from now on," said Stacio, inspecting Chestnut's mane. "Hey, Michael," he said, turning to face his son. "Why don't you play with your brothers?" he asked, grabbing Chestnut's brush from a nearby shelf.

"I was playing, Papa," he said, pulling the harmonica from his patched up dungarees.

Stacio smiled and began to brush Chestnut's mane. "Okay, Michael, that's good."

Inside the house Stacio's wife, Linda, was icing Michael's birthday cake. She was a petite and wholesome beauty. She had lines around her eyes when she smiled, but she looked younger than her age. Linda was a devout Catholic who was born to be a wife and mother. She was a great housekeeper and an even better cook. Stacio was a lucky man and he knew it.

Out in public, Linda was demure and soft-spoken. She wasn't shy, but she kept to herself and never got involved in any drama or gossip. Her strength and quiet confidence made her the envy of most women that knew her, but none of that ever mattered to Linda. What mattered most to her was keeping her beautiful boys happy and well-fed. That she did, spending most of her waking hours making homemade bread and jams when she wasn't cooking three meals a day from scratch.

Linda's kitchen was her domain; she jarred peaches in the fall and baked fresh pumpkin pies with every ingredient coming right from her own garden. In Linda's kitchen, she was a very different woman. She commanded the entire house from behind her apron, keeping everyone's chores and daily tasks in order. Linda was the glue that held everything together. She was the heart and soul of the Jasinski family.

She was joyful, kind, and very easy to please. Linda's most prized possessions were her family, her church, and her porcelain tea cups. She wasn't fancy or high maintenance by any means, but from the time she was a little girl she always collected tea cups. Her collection was impressive, most of which was displayed nicely in a tightly packed china cabinet, but her absolute favorites, the ones that meant the most to her, those were stacked neatly on custom shelving Stacio hung throughout the kitchen.

Every single night before bed she stood on a bench and smiled as she dusted them off. Those tea cups were Linda's pride and joy. If she ever offered you a cup of tea and you accepted, you were guaranteed to get your tea in a coffee mug. Linda's tea cups meant the world to her, and no one was to ever even think about putting a finger on them.

Grandpa came limping down the stairs, slow and steady, a seventy year old man who wasn't very hunched for his age. He wore a flannel shirt with black slacks and suspenders. He had glasses, a mustache, and a full head of white hair. He moved quick for an old man, snatching a dab of icing with his finger before Linda smacked his hand with the blade.

"Keep your paws off Michael's cake."

"Ouch," he said, licking the icing from his finger. "D-e-licious. I dare say it's worth the welt." He reached back out toward the cake and smiled. "One more little taste?"

Linda raised the blade again. "I wouldn't if I were you."

"Fine," he said, retreating from the kitchen with his head hung low.

"Dear, lord, come here," she said, handing him a spoon with the mixing bowl.

Grandpa refused the spoon and tilted the bowl to lick the rim.

"Pop, please use the spoon, we're not animals."

"Fine," he said, snatching the spoon and scraping it around the bowl.

"Come here," she said, taking the towel from her shoulder and dabbing Grandpa's ear. "You have shaving cream behind your ear again."

"I didn't shave today," he said, smiling at her disgust as he licked the spoon clean.

"Oh, dear God," she said, palming her forehead. "Please go get everyone while I find the candles."

"Will do," said Grandpa, walking out of the kitchen with the bowl in his hands.

A few moments later everyone was gathered in the kitchen, clapping as Michael blew out his candles.

"I hope you made a good wish," said Grandpa.

"I sure did," he replied.

Stevie handed Michael a small jewelry box. "Open mine first."

Michael opened it up and took out a sack of marbles. "Neat," he said. "Thanks, Stevie."

Stanley walked in front of Stevie with a large gift in his hands. "Forget the marbles, Michael, wait till you see this."

Michael tore the paper away to find a wooden stand. It looked like a small easel, but he had never seen one up close before. "What is it?"

Stanley took it from Michael. "Here, let me stand it up for you."

Michael looked at it and smiled. "What does it do?"

"It's for your music," said Stanley. "I made it myself."

Michael's eyes lit up when he realized what it was.

"You put your sheet music here when you play," said Stanley, pointing at the small shelf toward the top of the stand.

"I love it," said Michael, shivering with excitement. "Thank you so much, Stanley."

Michael looked at his mother, trying to stay calm. Linda had a concerned look on her face as she sliced the cake. She knew exactly what Michael thought he was getting, and she knew he wasn't getting it today. Michael's excitement died down after seeing his mother's expression.

Stacio handed Michael a box wrapped in a brown paper bag. "Go ahead, Michael."

Michael tore the paper apart and opened the box, holding up a baseball glove. He smiled politely, trying his best to hide his disappointment. "Thank you, Papa."

"Try it on," said Stacio, "it's already broken in."

Michael slid the glove on. It swallowed his tiny hand, but he smiled up at his father anyway.

"The next Stan Musial, huh?" said Grandpa, patting Stacio on the back.

Michael stood up and gave his father a kiss. "Thank you for my cake and all of my gifts."

"You're very welcome, sweetheart," Linda said, handing out slices of cake.

"Can we go play catch out front?" Stevie asked, with his mouth full.

"Stephen, your manners," said Linda.

"Sorry, Mama."

"It's all right," she said. "You can all go play after your cake."

Stevie swallowed before he spoke this time, "Thanks, Mama."

She smiled, but her smile faded when she looked at Michael. He was smiling, too, but Linda knew her son's real smile. So did Stacio.

Later that night, Linda and Stacio sat together on the living room sofa. Grandpa was across from them, rocking in his chair. They were all amazed by the soothing melody coming from the front porch. Michael's harmonica filtered through the old house like a lullaby. It was so calming that Linda and Grandpa closed their eyes to listen. Stacio just stared at the wall. He smiled at the music, but something inside was weighing on him.

"That boy is gifted," said Grandpa. "His harmonica cries. How could a boy of ten know that kind of heartache?"

"He must've heard it on the radio. He never forgets a song," said Linda.

Stacio leaned forward and looked down at the floor. He hunched over, rubbing his overworked hands.

"Linda," he said, softly.

"Yes, dear?"

"He didn't like his gift?"

"It's not that. He was just expecting something else."

"What?" he asked.

"Every time we pass Stroheim's store, Michael gawks at the violin in the window."

"A violin?"

"It's my fault, Stacio. He asks every single time we pass, so I told him, 'someday'. I shouldn't have done that, especially with his birthday so close. It was my mistake."

"How much does this violin cost?" he asked.

"Thirty dollars."

"Thirty dollars?"

"Yes."

Stacio didn't say anything, he just scooted in front of the coffee table and started cracking walnuts with his bare hands. He hid his emotions behind his ice blue eyes like he always did.

With one eye on his son, Grandpa struck a match to his tobacco pipe and blew out a thick cloud of smoke. He pondered for a moment, looking lost in his thoughts as he leaned back in his chair and closed his eyes.

Chapter Three

There goes the neighborhood

Gallagher's Pub was one of Stacio's first accounts. It was also one of the ugliest, hole-in-the-wall bars in Chicago. It was old and run down, but it was always packed with local drunks. Gallagher swore he'd never sell the place no matter the offer, but judging by the two men on ladders that were removing the sign from out front, someone had called his bluff.

Stacio went through the back with a huge block of ice. He leaned his shoulder into the keg room door and went inside. After a few minutes he came out and made his way to the bar. He grabbed a pint and walked up to the brass tap. The bar had a copper top with a dark wooden body. Irish flags were hanging over faded murals all around the room. A Celtic warrior wielding two swords in a tartan kilt was frescoed on the wall behind the bar.

The place stunk of spilt beer and pipe tobacco. The only food choices were pickled eggs or smoked whiting, because despite the large kitchen in the back, Gallagher was too damn cheap to hire a cook. If you listened closely, you could hear bagpipes coming from the radio behind the bar.

Like usual, there were a handful of odd locals with nowhere better to go, a few working men that were on their liquid lunch break, and a couple of drunks on their designated stools. Everybody at Gallagher's sat together, elbow to elbow, sipping their beers. Same as yesterday, same as tomorrow.

Two carpenters came up beside Stacio and started measuring the bar. Stacio stepped out of their way, filled his pint and took an empty stool next to Old Man Albert, a friendly local who knew Stacio well. Old Man Albert wore a wool cap and a flannel shirt. Since retiring fifteen years earlier, he'd spent nearly forty hours a week at Gallagher's, sipping beer on his own designated stool. Even when Albert wasn't there, which was rare, no one would ever dare sit in his spot.

"Right where I left you," said Stacio.

"I thought I felt a chill," said Albert.

Stacio chuckled and touched the back of the old man's neck.

"Christ, get those hands off me. You're cold as a tombstone."

"Cold hands, warm heart," said Stacio.

"Put your heart on my neck then, would ya? Keep those damn ice pops away from me."

They shared a laugh. Stacio leaned toward the old man when he saw a contractor pull large blueprints from a bag.

"What's going on around here, Albert?"

"The new owner's are fixing up the joint."

"I can't believe Gallagher sold the place," said Stacio, sipping his beer.

"He hadn't planned on it, but the cheap bastard got an offer he couldn't turn down."

"Must've been a heavy hitter."

"You got that right, Stash. It was the heaviest hitter."

Stacio looked up from his glass. "Ubano bought this place?"

"Nope," Albert laughed. "Heavier."

"Who's heavier than the mob?"

"Mr. Patty O'Banion himself." Albert flashed his toothless grin.

"The fighter?"

"Not just any fighter, Stash. The heavyweight champ bought this old joint."

Stacio just shrugged his shoulders and took another sip of his beer. He looked up when two men wrestled into the bar. The bigger guy had the smaller guy in a headlock, but the smaller guy was feisty and determined to break loose. They were like two bulls in a china shop, knocking over stools, causing a ruckus and annoying the hell out of the architect.

"Who are these goons?" Stacio asked.

"The O'Banion brothers," said Albert. "The big one's Richie and the humongous one's Kenny."

Kenny was the oldest of the three O'Banion brothers and he was also the biggest. He was nearly a giant at over six and a half feet tall. He was a mammoth of a man, barrel chested and thick all over. He was forty years old, but when you're one of three boys, especially close boys, you tend to stay a boy for life.

Richie broke out of the headlock and jumped on Kenny's back.

"Relax. Relax," Kenny yelled. "Come on, Richie, you pissed off the architect."

"Too bad," Richie yelled, sliding his forearm over Kenny's windpipe. "Say uncle."

At thirty years old, Richie was the middle brother. He was a big guy but he looked tiny next to Kenny, especially then, hanging onto Kenny's back with his feet dangling in the air. Richie was a wild man. He was fearless and had a short fuse, but he always managed to keep Patty out of trouble.

"Uncle. Uncle. Jesus, Richie," Kenny choked, tapping out on Richie's forearm.

Richie let go and jumped off his brothers back like a bull rider.

"You're a jackass," said Kenny. "That was a cheap shot."

"Yeah, yeah, yeah," said Richie.

The architect walked up, fuming. "Come on, guys, someone sign off on these damn prints already."

Kenny took a fake lunge at Richie. Richie flinched and his fists came up. "Easy, big fella."

"This ain't over, runt," Kenny said, smiling. "Sorry buddy," Kenny turned to the architect and wiped sweat from his forehead, "can't sign anything till the Champ gets back."

The architect rolled up his blueprints. He shook his head and snapped his pencil as he stormed away. Kenny and Richie looked at each other, giggling quietly.

"Kenny, did you see the way that pencil snapped?" Richie whispered. "Man's a beast."

Kenny laughed, making his way behind the bar as Richie turned and walked off, still laughing to himself. Kenny stood in front of Stacio and rolled up his sleeves. His forearms were covered in tattoos and they were the size of a normal man's legs.

"I'm sorry to tell you boys that we'll be closed tomorrow for renovations," he said, reaching for their empty glasses. "The Champ wants to pick up your tabs for today."

Kenny filled both glasses and slid them back where they were. Stacio nodded. Kenny nodded back at him.

"How long?" Albert asked.

"Don't know, but it's gonna be worth the wait," said Kenny, with a smirk on his face. "We're really gonna classy up the joint. You won't even be able to recognize it."

Kenny turned away from them and made his way down the bar.

Albert leaned toward Stacio and mumbled, "They better not raise the prices."

Stacio kept his eyes glued to his beer and said, "What's happened to our city, Albert? The old neighborhoods… they're all disappearing."

"Don't I know it," said Albert. "I still can't believe they're scrapping all the streetcars. It's a sin."

"It really is," said Stacio.

"Look at this work of Irish perfection," said Albert, sliding his stool back to stand up.

Stacio looked up. Patty O'Banion walked in from the back room with Richie clearing a path in front of him. Patty was the youngest of the three brothers. He was built like an action figure, his muscles seemed to have muscles of their own. He was a little bit bigger than Richie, but much smaller than Kenny. At twenty-five years old he was lean, and in much better shape than either of his brothers. He was in fighting shape. After all, he was the heavyweight champion of the world.

The music seemed to stop when Patty entered the room. Everyone in the bar looked in the Champ's direction. He was almost a majestic presence, dressed to the nines with a diamond ring shining from his pinky. Patty took a puff of his cigar and looked around the room. He was a handsome man despite his pug nose and cauliflower ears. His thick black curls were slicked back with lilac oil and his contagious smile showed off a mouthful of his own teeth. Patty seemed to have everything, especially charisma. Even if you wanted to hate him, you loved him. You couldn't help yourself. This kid had an unexplainable charm about him.

Everyone in the bar went over to greet the Champ, everyone except Stacio, who stayed in his seat and sipped his beer. People reached out to touch Patty, asking for autographs and handshakes. The architect pushed and squeezed his way to the front of the crowd holding the rolled-up blueprints over his head, even more annoyed than before.

Patty puffed his cigar and looked across the room. He noticed Stacio sitting alone at the bar, unfazed by his fame.

"This guy don't look like a drunk," Patty said to his brothers, pointing a thumb toward Stacio. "He don't know who I am?"

"Maybe he just don't give a damn," Richie laughed.

"Hahaha," Patty belted out a fake laugh. "Real funny, runt."

"The two of you with this runt thing," Richie said with a frown. "I'm a big guy. He's just a damn giant," he said, pointing at Kenny, "and you only got an inch on me."

"Yeah, keep telling yourself that," Patty laughed.

Kenny laughed, too, but Richie wasn't amused.

"That's the Iceman," said Kenny. "He don't say much."

Patty stared at Stacio, intrigued. The architect broke Patty's concentration when he waved the blueprints in his face.

"Everybody, grab a seat," Patty yelled. "Drinks are on the house."

Everyone cheered and scattered back to their stools.

"I need the green light, Patty," the architect said. "I've been paying guys to stand around all day."

"Relax," said Patty, puffing his cigar. "Follow me." He waved the architect along and walked across the room. He stopped and tapped on one of the columns. "I want this post gone." Then he turned and pointed to a second column on the other side of the room. "And I want that one gone, too."

"Patty, I already told you those are load bearing."

"They're gone," said Patty. "They're in the middle of my dance floor and I want them gone." Patty patted the architect on the back and took another puff of his cigar. "You'll figure it out."

Patty walked away from the architect and went behind the bar. His eyes were fixed on Stacio, but Stacio kept his eyes on his beer.

29

"Hey, shy-guy, is that your horse out back?" Patty asked.

Albert nudged Stacio. "The Champ, Stash. He's talking to you."

Stacio looked up from his glass, "Yes, yes it is."

"That's a fine looking animal," said Patty.

Stacio smiled and nodded. "Thank you."

Patty twisted his cigar into the ashtray. "I used to have a horse of my own. Beautiful, just like yours, but the damn thing never won me a single race," he said, leaning in with a smile on his face. "They told me it was because he was always constipated." Patty's smile grew wider as he anticipated the punchline. "Wanna know what I told them? I said, 'that sounds like horse shit to me.'" Patty burst out laughing. Kenny, Richie and Albert all laughed along with him.

Stacio just lifted his glass and took his last gulp. He set the glass down gently and flashed a light smile in the Champ's direction. Patty wasn't offended, but funny or not, he was accustomed to everyone in the room laughing at all of his corny jokes. Patty put his hand behind Kenny's head and brought his mouth to his brother's ear. His eyes stayed fixed on Stacio as he whispered something to Kenny.

"Take care, fellas," said Patty, walking out from behind the bar.

"Bye, Champ. Glad to have you in the neighborhood," said

Albert, raising his glass.

Kenny grabbed Stacio's empty glass and refilled it. "Hey, Iceman, today was your last delivery," he said, sliding the beer back to him.

"I understand," Stacio replied, closing his eyes and choking down another lost customer.

Kenny leaned in. "It's nuttin' personal, we're just modernizing," he said, turning to pour himself a beer. "Cheers, men."

All three men lifted their glasses to their mouths. Kenny and Albert both took a gulp, but Stacio chugged the whole pint. He pushed the empty glass away before standing up to put on his cap.

"You'll still come around, won't ya, Stash?" Albert asked.

Stacio forced a smile. "Sure, Albert, I'll be around."

"Take care, Iceman," Kenny said, lifting his glass to salute Stacio.

Stacio tipped his cap to Kenny and walked out.

Chapter Four

Gold has no memory, no conscience

Stacio was working up a sweat in the barn organizing tools and shoveling horse manure. He piled the last scoop into a wheelbarrow and leaned his pitchfork against the wall. He filled a pail with water and poured it into Chestnut's trough. "You're a good girl," he said, petting her softly as she drank.

Grandpa walked into the barn with a broom in his hands. Stacio turned to look at his father. "You come to clean up?" he asked.

Grandpa looked back at him and smiled. "Something like that," he said, sweeping hay away from a concealed basement hatch. "Come with me, Stacio."

Grandpa groaned as he bent down and reached for the handle.

"No, let me," said Stacio, helping Grandpa get upright before pulling the hatch open.

Stacio jumped in first and guided Grandpa down the dangerously steep staircase. They swatted at spiders and cobwebs as they descended deeper into the catacomb cellar. It was a long, dank basement with twisting strings of lamps running along both sides. Below the lamps, oak barrels lined every wall.

"I used to love coming down here to escape the summer heat," said Grandpa.

Stacio sat on one of the two stools in front of an old butcher block table. Grandpa walked over to one of the barrels, tapped a spigot and poured beer into a pitcher. Then he sat down and reached under the table, pulling out two silver steins. He filled them both to the top.

"How's business?" he asked, sliding one of the steins to Stacio.

"Not good, Pop."

Grandpa sipped his beer. "Talk to me about it."

"Just… competition," said Stacio.

"Who? Is it the Zielinski brothers?"

"No," said Stacio, sipping his beer. "It's this electric refrigerator."

"Ahh, machines break down," said Grandpa. "When they do, they'll need your ice again."

"I don't know, Pop. Things have changed so fast, I just can't keep up."

Grandpa looked for the right words to say, but they were nowhere to be found. He knew Stacio was smart enough to realize his profession was becoming more useless as the years went on. Time had finally left him behind, and although he was one hell of a worker, he was always too stubborn to admit defeat. Grandpa took a deep breath, fighting to hold his tears at bay.

"I never wanted this for you, Stacio. You're an iceman to your bones, but we told you that it would never be an easy life."

Stacio shook his head and held up a hand. "Please, Pop, don't."

"Your brother chose the priesthood and that made your mother proud," said Grandpa, reaching under his glasses to dry his eyes. "But you, Stacio, she always thought you would be an engineer. I thought so, too. You always had the mind for it."

Stacio sipped his beer. "I'm good with my hands, Pop. That's all." He set his stein down and took a deep breath. "Besides, no one can change the past."

"Look around, Stacio, this… this is all the past." Grandpa stood up. "I sold a hundred barrels a week. Moran's gang, Capone, Hymie Weiss. Those men paid me every single week. I made a lot of money,

Stacio, and they always paid. They always paid because the ale was scarce, and because my ale was great. But those good days will never come back. You must figure out what the people need, figure out what they need and give it to them. They will pay for what they need, son."

"Those men were criminals, Pop. Murderers."

"The law is for suckers, Stacio. Those men were the ones who really protected us. Made sure we were never cheated."

"I know, Pop, I know. Honor among thieves. Right?"

"At least you knew what you were getting," said Grandpa, prying the lid away from one of his oak barrels. He lifted out a string and untied a wet canvas bag from the opposite end. He reached inside the bag and slammed two gold coins on the table in front of Stacio. "Isn't it amazing how gold never corrodes?" he asked.

Stacio pushed the coins away. As bad as he needed them and as much as they would help, he would never accept his father's money, 'dirty money' as he always thought of it.

"No, Pop, put those back."

"Please, just take these coins and go buy your boy that violin," Grandpa begged. "He deserves it."

"I know he does," said Stacio. "I'll get it for him the right way."

"What is this right way?" Grandpa scoffed. "Don't be ridiculous, Stacio, just take the coins. They're a gift from me to you, from a father to his son."

"I can't. I'll find another way."

"Can't you put your pride aside just this one time?" Grandpa begged. "Gold has no memory, no conscience. It all spends the same."

"I do, Pop. I have a memory and a conscience. Thank you, but no."

"So stubborn, so proud," said Grandpa, dropping the coins back into the barrel. "I can't say I don't know where you get that from. I know you won't budge, but you know where the coins are if you do."

Chapter Five

Twelve cents an hour

The next morning when Stacio walked into Michael's room he had a

bit more pep in his step than he had in the last few days. The sun

hadn't come up yet, but the Iceman was ready for work. He leaned in

and nudged a sleeping Michael.

"Wake up, boy, time to make money," he said, smiling.

Michael's room was in the attic, he was the last born so he got

the leftover space. He didn't mind, though, because being on his own

floor meant no one bothered him about his harmonica, which he

seemed to play from dusk until dawn.

The room was small, packed with mismatched furniture and old

steamer chests. Michael's bed was against the wall in the far corner.

Linda's old nightstand and reading lamp sat tight to the left side of

the bed frame. Stacio reached out and turned on the lamp. A small,

octagon window sat half way up the wall to the right of Michael's headboard. Stacio stood there a moment, staring into the sky.

"Papa?" Michael said, still half asleep.

Stacio looked back to his son. "Get dressed, quick, we should have left already."

Michael stood in front of the conveyor belt at Degan's Icehouse. He looked nervous as large blocks of ice crept toward him in a single file line. Stacio walked up and set down his clipboard.

"Bend your knees, Michael, never lift with your back."

Stacio grabbed the frozen blocks with his bare hands and tossed them in the carriage like they were five pounds instead of seventy-five pounds. Michael reached out and pulled his hands back. Even with his thickest mittens on he could barely stand the arctic burn, it came through every layer and stung the bones in his tiny hands. Michael's teeth chattered as he looked up at his father in amazement. *Wow, my papa's tough,* he thought. *My papa's tougher than John Wayne.*

The icehouse was always freezing inside, it had to be. The cold never bothered Stacio, especially at this point in his life. He actually preferred it. He was immune, but he knew the icehouse was no place for the warm-blooded, especially a warm-blooded child like Michael.

Sometimes even Chestnut refused to go inside, so he'd have to

unhook her outside and drag the carriage in and out by himself.

"Too cold?" he asked his son.

Michael forced his teeth to stop chattering long enough to tell a

white lie, "No, Papa," he said, grabbing a block of ice and struggling

with its weight, temperature, and size. He leaned it on the ledge of

the carriage and shoved it inside with two hands and all of his might.

"Good job, Michael," said Stacio, smiling and patting his son's

head.

Later that day Stacio, Michael, and Chestnut rode up to Rudy's

Bowling Alley. Stacio pulled off to the side of the road and looked at

his son.

"Always look first, Michael. These motorcars move far too fast

to stop."

"Yes, Papa."

Just as Stacio turned in his seat to look back, a car sped past

them.

"Pierce Arrow," said Michael.

"Yes, that's good," Stacio said, hopping out and running to the back of the carriage before the next car reached them.

The next car passed. "And that one?" Stacio asked as his son walked up.

"Studebaker."

Stacio nodded his head in approval as a group of cars came speeding up. Michael slid his harmonica into his pocket and looked close. "Caddy, Packard, Arrow, Caddy, and… Dodge. I think that last one was a Dodge, Papa." Michael leaned into the street to see the back of the last car, "Yup, definitely a Dodge."

"Very good, Michael, very good."

Stacio was impressed, looking on and seeing that his son got a perfect score, even on the Dodge. Another car laid on the horn as it whipped by.

"Get back," Stacio yelled, yanking Michael out of the street by his arm. "These motorcars will run you over, Michael. Stay off the street. Always."

"Sorry, Papa."

"It's okay, just be more careful."

"I will."

Stacio came into the bowling alley with a huge block of ice

gripped in his metal tongs. Michael followed close behind him like a puppy. Stacio turned to look at his son. "I want to introduce you to someone, Michael."

"Okay, Papa."

It was a modest bowling alley, but it had everything you needed for a good time. There was a handful of lanes, a small bar and a food cart with a large grill. You could hear bowling balls slamming and rumbling down wooden lanes and pins colliding and ricocheting into the pit. But the smell of hot dogs, cheeseburgers and French fries, that smell was the best part. Stacio loved delivering ice to Rudy's. Michael seemed to like it, too. Stacio actually caught him smiling as he looked around and took in the atmosphere.

"You like this place?" he asked his son.

"I do, Papa."

"Good," said Stacio, resting the ice on the top of his boot.

Rudy stood across the bar with a white rag on his shoulder. "How are you, Stash?"

"I'm well, and you?"

"Ehh, can't complain," said Rudy. "Set that down and have a beer with me."

Stacio walked around the bar and set the block of ice in the old wooden ice box. "Go look around, Michael, but stay in sight."

"Okay, Papa," he said, running off to inspect the rest of the bowling alley.

"Pretty quick kid," said Rudy. "He's your youngest?"

Stacio nodded.

"He's small," said Rudy, filling two glasses with beer, "but he has plenty of time to sprout up. You know how boys sprout up."

Stacio pulled up a stool. Rudy slid one of the beers to him and took a sip from the other.

"He's frail, Rudy, he can't work with me. He'll get hurt and Linda will be angry. I would be angry with myself if anything happened." Stacio took a sip of his beer. "Besides, the icehouse is too cold for him."

"Stash, that icehouse is too cold for a damn polar bear," said Rudy, taking a sip from his own beer.

The two men shared a laugh.

"What are you thinking, Stash?" asked Rudy.

"Could you give him a job? He's a good worker, he'll keep up. I give you my word."

Rudy took another sip of his beer and looked across the alley to spot Michael, who was rolling two bowling balls into each other and smiling.

"He's pretty fast, I guess. I could use another pinsetter," said Rudy, "but it's a night shift. Five-to-ten."

Stacio thought about it for a moment, "Ten seems late for a boy."

"Yeah, it is pretty late, but it's all I got, Stash. Twelve cents an hour."

Stacio nodded and stood up, reaching across the bar to shake Rudy's hand. "He'll take it. Thank you."

"No," said Rudy, "Thank you."

Michael did move fast, and to Rudy's pleasant surprise he was a great worker, just as Stacio promised. *He's even better than Stacio promised,* Rudy thought.

Michael shuffled around, grabbing and setting pins on their marks. He was the youngest and smallest pinsetter so he had to work a bit harder than the rest of the boys. Sweat fell from his brow as he outworked everyone around him. Michael looked over and saw Rudy keeping a close eye on his workers. Rudy smiled at Michael and gave him a thumbs-up. Michael smiled back and wiped the sweat from his eyes before getting back to work.

Michael walked out of the bowling alley, his shift was over and it was a dark night.

"Michael, over here," Stacio yelled, waving from his carriage across the lot.

Michael turned and walked toward his father. He dragged his feet, the boy was exhausted. He glanced down a dim lit alley as he passed. A few teenage boys rolled dice against the wall as they did most nights before heading home. A red-headed boy from the bunch looked up and pointed at Stacio's wagon.

"Take a look, guys, it's the Lone Ranger."

The boys all looked up from their dice and laughed. Stacio just tipped his cap and grabbed Chestnut's reins. Michael would never say so, but Stacio knew that for the first time in his son's young life, he was embarrassed by his father, or at least by his father's means of transportation.

"Where's Grandpa?" Michael asked. "He always picks me up in the truck."

"He fell asleep."

"Again?"

"Yes," said Stacio. "Did you finish your homework?"

"I did, Papa."

"Good, keep your grades up or no job. Understand?"

"Yes, Papa," he said, taking out his harmonica. "May I?"

"Of course, Michael." Stacio smiled at his son as he lifted
Chestnut's reins. "Let's go home, girl," he said, and with a gentle
whip of his wrists, they were off. Stacio steered, Chestnut trotted,
and Michael played his heart out the entire ride home.

A few months later, Michael came home from work and ran
directly to his room. "I think I have enough," he yelled, storming up
the stairs. He emptied his pockets onto the bed and dumped his piggy
bank upside down. He smiled at the pile, grabbing coins and stacking
them onto his nightstand.

A few minutes later, Linda peaked into the room. "Get to bed,
Michael, it's late."

"Okay, Mama," he said, grabbing the coins and sliding them
back into his piggy bank.

"Michael," Linda spoke softly, leaning farther into the room, "don't be disappointed if Stroheim already sold the violin. If he did, we'll find you another one. I promise."

"It's still there, Mama, I just saw it," he said. "I check every single night when we ride by. It's right there in the big window."

"That's wonderful news," said Linda, entering the room and kissing him on the head. "Goodnight, Michael. I love you."

"Goodnight, Mama. I love you, too," he said, setting his piggy bank on the dresser and changing into his pajamas. Michael slipped under his covers and was nearly asleep before his head hit the pillow.

"Sleep tight," said Linda, switching off the light and pulling the door closed.

Chapter Six

A splendid establishment

Autumn was on its last leaf, and the grand opening of Patty

O'Banion's nightclub was underway. He called the newly renovated

spot, 'Patty's Place', and the blinking neon sign out front was just as

obnoxious as the name. The bar was so packed that bouncers and

police officers were outside turning people away.

Everyone at Patty's Place looked sharp, even the people that

couldn't get in. The women wore sexy sequin dresses with their

finest jewelry. The men wore suits, fedora hats, and freshly shined

shoes. It was quite the festive atmosphere. This building, formally

known as Gallagher's, had never dreamed of these types of people

walking through its doors, but there they were, and there was Patty

O'Banion himself.

'Midnight Serenade' played through the entire building, and

Patty seemed to float through the place in his pearl white suit. He

smiled when he pointed up at the giant 'Have a drink with The

Champ' banner that ran along the back wall. He joined his brothers behind the bar, set down his cigar and started pouring shots.

"Line up, folks, line up. Patty's Place has the best giggle water in all of Chicago."

Patty's smile lit up the room as he looked around and took in the atmosphere. He sure was in his element. Anyone with eyes could have told you that. Not only was Patty the heavyweight champion of the world, he was also a celebrity. The bar was filled with big jazz musicians, noted athletes, mobsters, actors and novelists, but nobody in that building was more famous than Patty O'Banion. People came from all over the country for this grand opening, but they mostly came just to be around him, just to get a taste of that charisma.

Patty was born to be in the ring, it came naturally to him so he ran with it. He'd promised himself he wouldn't labor his life away like his father had, he would find a smarter way to feed his family. Believe it or not, he never really wanted to be a professional fighter, he just used boxing as a platform to help him reach his ultimate goal. Patty's dream was to open a chain of bars in all the biggest cities in the world. He wanted to create an atmosphere that everybody wanted to be a part of. A place where he could be the center of attention and provide his guests with top of the line everything.

Patty wanted a place where a hard-working man, like his father, could go for a drink after a long day of work. A place that converted into the fanciest nightclub anyone had ever seen once the sun went down. This grand opening was a big part of Patty's dream, and by the look on his face, you could tell he was living it.

A photographer nudged his way to the front of the bar and stopped directly in front of Patty. "Smile, Champ," he yelled, snapping a picture. Flash bulbs popped from every direction. Patty lifted up his gem-studded, championship belt and bared his teeth to the cameras. More flashes came from all around. The crowd cheered and applauded, the place was in an uproar. He lifted his fist to Kenny, more bulbs flashed. He turned and lifted his fist to Richie, the popping and flashing continued.

Patty's manager eased the photographer back a few feet and took his spot next to the Champ. Marty Spiegel was pushing sixty, he wore bifocals and a Brooks Brothers suit. He'd been Patty's manager since the start, and though it wasn't always easy, he knew exactly how to handle his young champion. "Any questions for the Champ?" he asked the crowd.

Kenny pressed his fingers to his mouth and whistled. The crowd calmed down for a moment and a reporter stepped forward. "When's your next fight, Champ?"

"Don't know," said Patty, shrugging his shoulders. "Can't find any volunteers."

The whole crowd laughed. Marty smiled and nodded his head like a proud father. Marty hit the jackpot when he took a huge gamble on O'Banion. Against everyone's collective advice, Marty risked his entire career to help groom the wildman everyone else had shied away from.

Just before Patty went pro, the Chief Editor of boxing's most prestigious magazine, The Ring, had this to say about him, "O'Banion is the most gifted raw talent boxing has seen since Rodney Chambers took the sport by storm in 1942. As strong, fast, and powerful as O'Banion is, his lack of discipline and professionalism will not only hold him back, but will taint the careers of everyone associated with him. O'Banion's sense of entitlement and reckless abandon is a disaster waiting to happen. The boxing commision has zero tolerance for tomfoolery, and will be watching him like a hawk. Don't be blinded by the man's gold plated potential.

Proceed with caution.".

After a few run-ins with the law, Patty was written off as a disciplinary case with character issues, but Marty was a sucker for raw talent, and Patty had an abundance of it. Nobody in the boxing world had ever seen anything like O'Banion in the ring. He was so vicious, fearless, and unstoppable, completely dominating everyone that stood across from him. Marty took a leap of faith, and it paid off big time.

Patty O'Banion was Marty's biggest accomplishment, and he knew the Champ would be the cornerstone of his legacy for generations. He loved him like a son, but he mostly loved him like a good investment. "We'll find somebody who's not scared of him soon enough," said Marty. "I promise you that."

"I sure hope so," Patty said, shrugging his shoulders. "I ain't gettin' any younger over here."

"Let me see," said Marty, pointing around the crowd. "Anybody here wanna fight him? It'll hurt, but it'll be a nice pay-day."

The crowd laughed.

"Maybe I should retire," said Patty. "This hooch peddling business is a whole lot easier."

Marty spun around and looked at him. "And what," he said, "kick your manager to the curb?"

Everyone in the bar laughed again, including Marty and Patty. Loud swing music ended at the exact same time the crowd stopped laughing, and for that short moment, the entire place heard the sweet sound of a grand piano. On the far side of the club, tucked into the corner, there was a small piano lounge overflowing with people. The entire crowd was impressed when they heard the beautiful music, but no one was really there to listen to the sounds of Chopin's 'Nocturne'. People were there to party, drink, and hang out with Patty O'Banion.

In unison, every single person in Patty's Place turned and gawked at the incredible pianist. Everyone there was undoubtedly impressed, but her music would have been much more appreciated in another atmosphere. Molly O'Banion stroked the keys so gracefully. She played with her eyes closed, focused, allowing the vibrations from the keyboard to enter through her fingertips and dance around inside her beautiful mind. She was twenty-five years old, elegant and gorgeous. She had her chic, black hair pinned back in a fancy up-do. She wore a svelte gown, and her jewelry was a perfect mix of pearls and diamonds. She was the definition of a lady, and she was damn near flawless.

"Molly. Aye, Moll," Patty yelled across the room, "you trying to put everybody to sleep? They can't buy drinks if they're sleepin'."

Molly looked up and realized the whole place was staring at her. She pulled her hands away from the keys and gently closed the fallboard. Molly was a shy, modest woman. She forced a smile and slid away from the piano.

"Hey, Moll." Patty waved her over. "Come get in the pictures."

"Yeah," the crowd clapped and cheered. "Take some pictures."

Molly was bashful, she didn't like the spotlight the way her husband did.

"No, Patty," she giggled, waving him off.

"Come on, Moll, please."

Molly smiled and shook her head. "Patty, stop it."

"Don't make me beg, gal. I'll do it," said Patty, jumping up on the bar. He looked around the room and started to pump his fist and chant, "Mo-lly, Mo-lly, Mo-lly."

Richie and Kenny joined in, then Marty, then the entire bar, "Mo-lly, Mo-lly, Mo-lly."

Molly put her hand over her mouth and scanned the room, there was nowhere to run. *I'm gonna kill him*, she thought, her cheeks turning bright red.

"Hey, photo guy," said Patty, pointing to one of the photographers before he jumped off the bar. "Come get a shot of me and my wife."

The crowd went crazy when Patty picked Molly up in his strong arms. Every time a camera flashed, the crowd cheered louder.

"Put me down, you big ox." She wasn't mad, just bashful. When her feet touched the ground, she straightened out her dress and raised a stern finger. "You're in trouble when we get home, Mister."

"Promise?" Patty smiled and leaned in for a kiss.

"Jeez, Louise," Molly laughed, pecking him on the lips before pushing him away. "What am I going to do with you?"

Later that night, Michael emerged from the side door of Rudy's bowling alley. He was exhausted, dragging his feet as he walked. His shift was finally over and he earned every single penny he made. He looked around the parking lot, but Grandpa's truck was nowhere to be found. Michael shook his head and mumbled, "Come on,

Grandpa, not again." He bent down and grabbed a milkcrate, pushing it tight against the brick wall before taking a seat. He slid his harmonica out of his pocket, pressed it to his lips, and began to play.

Back at the farmhouse, Grandpa was sound asleep in his chair with a silver flask peeking out from his breast pocket. 'The Lone Ranger' played through an old Emerson radio with yellow knobs. The program had just ended, running through its final credits before eight solid hours of unbearable static. The radio went silent for a moment, then white noise yanked Grandpa from his sleep. He clutched the arm rests and sat up. "Jesus, Mary, and Joseph," he gasped, flipping his pocket watch open. He had to hold it an inch from his face and squint his eyes to read it. "Oh, God. Michael."

Grandpa jumped up from his chair, grabbed his jacket, and shuffled out of the house.

Linda sprang from her sleep when the screen door slammed shut. "Stacio," she said, shaking her husband.

Stacio lifted his head and opened one eye. "What is it, dear?"

"I'm worried about Michael," she said. "I have the most terrible feeling… and your father's just left."

"Is he late?" Stacio asked.

"Yes. Over an hour."

"Over an hour?" Stacio tossed off his covers and got out of the bed.

###

A full moon hung over Patty's Place. All the lights were out and there were only two cars left in the parking lot. The grand opening was over, and everything went as perfect as Patty had always dreamed it would. It was late, the bar was empty, the floor was sticky, kegs were tapped, stools were flipped, and Patty was holding the car door open for his beautiful wife.

"Congratulations," she said, kissing his cheek before climbing into the passenger seat.

"Thanks, Babe," he said, closing the door to his black, 1932 Duesenberg convertible. He waved to his brothers as he stumbled around to the driver side door.

"Take it slow, Champ," said Kenny.

"I got it," Patty said, jumping in the car, slamming the door, and peeling out of the parking lot.

"Jesus, Patty," Kenny mumbled, shaking his head.

###

Back at Rudy's, Michael was still sitting in the alley, playing his music under the stars. He stopped and looked down at his harmonica, studying it from plate to plate. "I'll still play you when I get my violin," he said, reassuring his trusty, old instrument. "I promise I will."

He stood up and walked to the edge of the road. He looked both ways, but there was no sign of Grandpa's headlights. Michael continued playing his harmonica as he wandered along the sidewalk, kicking rocks and jumping over cracks. By the time he realized it, he'd already walked three blocks. He looked up and smiled, sliding the harmonica into his pocket.

Stroheim's store, he thought, sprinting the rest of the way with a huge smile on his face. He cupped his hands to the glass and peered into the antique shop. The violin was still there, waiting patiently for him to save enough money. At least, that's what Michael believed.

"It's beautiful," he whispered to himself.

###

Patty was driving decent for the amount he'd drank, but Molly still had to guide the steering wheel from time to time.

"Chilly night," she said, nuzzling up under Patty's arm. She reached out to help him steer straight.

"Let go of the wheel, Moll, I've driven tanks a lot bigger than this little roadster."

"Ok, dear, but slow down," she said. "What's the hurry?"

Patty reached under his seat, he pulled out a bottle of scotch and took a hefty swig. "Ahh, wasn't the bar grand, Molly?"

"It is a splendid establishment, dear. I'm very proud of you."

"You know, Moll," he said, taking a hard look at his wife. "You're so elegant and fine. What's a spiffy broad like you doing with a thug like me, anyhow?"

She smiled at him and guided the wheel to the right.

"Sing for me, Molly," he said. "Please."

"How about another time?"

"You better get to singing, little lady," Patty laughed. "Or else."

"Oh, dear. Or else, what?" she asked, pushing the wheel back toward the left.

"Or else... I'll play the victrola. I'll play the victrola all night long," he said, leaning over for a kiss.

"Keep your eyes on the road, Patty, and slow it down," she

yelled. "You're way over the lines."

Headlights flashed around the corner, coming straight at them. Patty looked up and yanked the wheel. The Duesenberg swerved back into its lane and slid across the dirt shoulder. They just barely grazed a telephone pole as they hopped the curb and bounced up onto the sidewalk.

"Hold on, Moll," Patty screamed, reaching his arm across her like a protective mother.

Michael turned away from his precious violin when he heard Patty's tires squeal. His eyes grew wide as he gasped, his body frozen with fear. The fender of Patty's convertible swatted Michael aside and crashed through the front of Stroheim's store. Glass exploded in every direction as Michael skidded across the concrete. Pain surged through his tiny body, but before he could scream, everything went black.

Molly caught a glimpse of a small silhouette just before she smashed into the dashboard. Her body ricocheted back into the seat, her head whipping hard on her neck. She took a moment to gather herself, brushing the hair out of her face. She sprung forward and screamed when she spotted Michael.

"Oh my God," said Molly, jumping out of the car and running to him. "He's just a boy," she cried.

"A boy," Patty mumbled, dazed. "What's a kid doing out here?"

Mr. Stroheim came shuffling up in his slippers. He was an old man, dressed in pajamas and a nightcap.

"My store. What did you do to my store?"

"Forget your store," Molly yelled, taking the shawl from her shoulders and sliding it behind Michael's head. "Call someone. Now."

When Stroheim spotted Michael on the ground, he turned and shuffled home. "I'll call right away."

Michael was in shock. He looked around, groggy. "Grandpa?"

"It's gonna be okay, sweetheart," Molly said, brushing the glass off Michael's shirt. "Help's on the way."

Patty was also in shock, he never even got out of the Duesenberg. "What's he doing out so late, Moll," he slurred, his words barely recognizable. "Ask him why he's in the middle of the street." Patty just sat there, he clutched his steering wheel and stared at his bloody teeth in the rearview mirror. *This is bad, Marty's gonna kill me.*

Chapter Seven

The cover-up

Two young police officers pushed Patty's car off the curb. The captain was a fat Irishman in his fifties. He stood in the middle of the street, pointing around and barking orders. "Seal the roads and block the damn sidewalk. I don't want anyone coming through here," he yelled, looking at a handful of younger cops. "Get Charlie out here to fix the glass. Tell him to get quick about it, I don't need those weasels from the Tribune showing up and asking questions."

Molly sat on the curb with Michael's head in her lap, he was barely conscious, pleading to her in Polish. She nodded and rubbed his head. She understood what he was saying. She understood many languages, Molly was an educated woman.

"What's that kid saying?" the captain asked.

"He wants his grandfather, and he's in a lot of pain." Molly said.

"What's going on? Why haven't you called the hospital? Where in the world is the ambulance?"

The captain took a deep breath and gritted his teeth. "All right, all right, I'll call Saint Barnabas."

"What? Why," Molly asked. "That's all the way on the Southside. There's a hospital five blocks from here."

"Relax, Mrs. O'Banion." The captain held out his hands. "He belongs at Saint Barnabas with his own. That's where all the Poles go."

Molly looked down at Michael and shook her head, she took out a silk handkerchief and wiped the tears from her eyes. "Help will be here very soon, sweetheart, I promise."

When the ambulance finally arrived, they didn't ask a single question. They just tossed Michael on a stretcher, loaded him up, and drove away. Molly wanted to ride with him, but Patty and the captain talked her out of it. They knew it would raise too many dicey questions at the hospital. She was still sitting on the curb, sobbing, while Patty stood behind her and rubbed her shoulders.

"I didn't see the kid, Moll, I swear it."

One of the young officers handed the unsealed bottle of scotch to the captain. "This was on the driver seat, Sir. It's almost empty."

"Get rid of it," he said, handing it back to the officer. "Quick."

The captain walked over and put an arm arm around Patty.

"Come on, Champ, let's get you home. We'll take care of everything here."

Molly looked up, disgusted and embarrassed as Patty stumbled to the car.

"I didn't see him, Cap, honest. I didn't see the kid."

"Don't worry, Champ. None of us seen the kid," said the captain. "None of us seen anything that happened here tonight."

Molly shook her head, appalled.

"Come on, Mrs. O'Banion," the captain said, reaching his hand out to help her up. "We did all we can do for the boy."

She refused his help and stood on her own. "Yeah, you both did plenty."

Molly walked to the passenger door of the Duesenberg and got in the back seat with Patty. She slid as far away from him as she could get, but he was still so drunk and stunned, he didn't even notice. One of the young officers got behind the wheel and drove them away.

The captain walked across the alley toward Mr. Stroheim, shaking in his pajamas. *There's a shit storm coming,* the captain thought. Mr. Stroheim looked overly frazzled when the captain got close enough to see his face.

"Shake it off, Stroheim," he said, "the glazier's on his way to fix your window. Send the bill to Precinct Nine for whatever your damages cost." The captain took another step toward him and poked a finger into the old man's chest. "Don't get greedy, either. I know how you old Jews operate."

Mr. Stroheim swallowed hard and nodded his head. "Yes, sir."

The captain leaned in closer, almost nose to nose with Stroheim. "By the way," he said, gripping his billy club, "you didn't see nuttin."

"Understood," Stroheim said, quivering.

"Hey, Stroheim," the captain took a step back, still clutching his weapon, "what happened here tonight? What happened to your store?"

"Nothing, Captain, I didn't see anything at all."

"Good."

Grandpa finally pulled up to the bowling alley, he slammed on the brakes and jumped out of the truck. "Michael," he hollered, into the night. "Where are you, Michael?"

He banged on Rudy's door, but there was no use, there hadn't
been anyone inside for quite a while. Grandpa walked into the alley
next to Rudy's, the same alley the teenage boys used for gambling
after work. The same alley where the boys pointed and laughed at the
Iceman who still used a horse and buggy, like he was making
deliveries in the Wild West. But even those boys were long gone,
asleep, tucked into their beds hours ago.

Grandpa weaved in and out of each dark alley, calling out,
searching desperately for his missing grandson. Cats hissed, rats
scurried, and bums snored, but Michael wasn't in any of these alleys.
Michael was nowhere near here, he was all the way on the Southside.
He was at Saint Barnabas – 'It's where all the poles go' as the fat
Irish captain put it - he was lying in a hospital bed, and he was all by
himself.

Grandpa had no idea what happened up to that point, but when he
spotted Mr. Stroheim sweeping up glass in front of his store,
Grandpa knew. It was instant, like how a mother knows something's
happened with her child before the child says anything about it,
sometimes, even before it happens at all. It's like a sixth sense that
we've all felt at one time or another, and Grandpa felt it, he felt it so

strong his knees almost buckled.

The hair stood up on the back of his neck, and his stomach flopped so hard he had to bring his hand to his mouth to keep from vomiting. *Oh my God, Michael.*

Grandpa ran over to Stroheim. "What happened here, Stroh?"

"Nothing happened."

Stroheim wouldn't look at Grandpa. He turned his head and shuffled into the store.

"Stroh," said Grandpa, catching the door and forcing his way in, "have you seen my grandson? Have you seen Michael?"

"No."

"Are you sure? He's the small one. A good boy."

Stroheim looked away, he held his breath and covered his mouth. He controlled his emotions well, but he couldn't speak at the risk of crying.

"Tell me what happened here," said Grandpa.

"Rocks," he said, clearing his throat and trying to sound more confident. "Crazy kids were throwing rocks."

Grandpa had been around those blocks far too many times to fall for such a terribly rehearsed answer. "Rocks did this, huh?" he asked, taking a better look at the damaged showcase. "A wrecking ball would be more believable."

"Please, Stanley, just go home," Stroheim begged, struggling to hold back his tears.

Grandpa ran both hands through his hair, fighting back tears of his own. He approached Mr. Stroheim slowly, forcing him to make eye contact. "Stroh, how long have I known you? Thirty years?"

"More." Stroheim's voice trembled.

Grandpa took a deep breath as he scanned the shop from left to right. He squinted his eyes, struggling to focus until his gaze locked on something across the room. Chills crept from the crown of his head all the way down the back of his heels when he spotted a broken violin sitting atop an old steamer chest. *That's it,* he thought, tears blurring his vision. *That's Michael's violin.* It was completely destroyed; the fingerboard was torn from the bout, and splinters were sprawled all across its wooden body. That old violin would never make music again, but its tattered strings were still holding strong, still keeping everything together in one piece.

Grandpa dried his eyes with his sleeve and placed a hand on his old friend's shoulder. "The boy, Stroh, my grandson. Where is he?"

Stroheim removed his nightcap and squeezed it with both hands. "I'm so sorry, Stanley," he said, bowing his head to Grandpa as he began to cry. "They took him to Saint Barnabas."

Grandpa ran up the farmhouse steps, rumbled through the front door, and went straight to the kitchen. He was so out of breath he couldn't talk for a moment. Linda popped up from the kitchen table with her rosary clutched to her heart. Stacio, dressed in work clothes, stopped pacing and looked up at Grandpa with bloodshot eyes. "Where is he?"

"There's been... an accident... a motorcar." Grandpa rested his hands on his knees, panting.

"Where is he?" Linda cried.

"He's at Saint Barnabas," said Grandpa. "He's alive."

Chapter Eight

Motorcars shouldn't be so fast

Michael was lying in a hospital bed with his eyes closed tight. Both of his legs were wrapped in casts that ran from his feet all the way up to his waist. Linda sat on the edge of his bed and cried quietly, still holding a rosary tight to her chest. Grandpa and Stacio, both silent, were sitting on metal chairs at the foot of the bed. Father Henry was holding Michael's hand, kneeling down on the floor with his eyes closed and his head bowed.

Father Henry was the priest at the Jasinski family's church. He was also very close to Michael because he was Stacio's older brother. He finished his silent prayer and got to his feet. He crossed himself with the Holy Trinity and kissed his nephew's hand. A nun came into the room with a wet cloth and dabbed Michael's forehead.

"Thank you," Michael whispered.

Everyone in the room looked up in amazement. "He speaks," Linda cried, scooting closer to her son. "Michael, my love." She grabbed onto his hand. "Are you in pain?"

Stacio hid his face with his arm as tears ran down both of his cheeks.

"No," said Michael. "I'm all right, I guess."

Stacio stood up, dried his face, and walked over to his son. He ruffled his boy's hair and smiled at him. "What happened, Michael?" he asked, in a stern tone.

"I tried to run, Papa, but it was too fast," he said, looking around Stacio to find Grandpa. "You were right, Grandpa, motorcars shouldn't be so fast."

"That's right, Michael," Grandpa replied, getting choked up when he tried to speak. "That's… that's right."

Grandpa turned away to wipe the tears from his eyes. He was so filled with guilt, he could barely look at his grandson in that hospital bed.

"Why were you in the street, son?" Stacio asked.

"I wasn't, Papa. Honest."

"Michael, tell the truth," said Stacio, looking disappointed.

It was hard for him to believe his son because Michael was notorious for being yanked out of the street by his mother, his father, his grandpa, and even his older brothers.

He got lost in his music and wandered into the street. I know it, Stacio thought to himself. *That boy would wander right off a cliff with that harmonica in his mouth.*

"Are you sure you're telling the truth, son?"

"I am, Papa."

Father Henry grabbed Stacio's arm and said, "Be grateful, brother, it's a miracle we didn't lose the boy."

Grandpa looked up at his sons with guilty eyes and nodded in agreement. "He's right."

Stacio turned and wrapped his arms around Michael. He kissed him on the head and said, "We're just happy that you're okay."

"You believe me, though, don't you?" Michael asked, looking back and forth at his parents.

"Yes. We believe you, dear," said Linda. "Are you thirsty? Can I get you anything?"

"I'd like my harmonica," he said.

Linda smiled, she looked over to the nun and nodded. The nun lifted Michael's bag of clothes and dug through it.

"Here you are, Michael," the nun said, "not too loud, though."

James Masse

Michael took the harmonica from her and started to play. He played like he always had, just a bit quieter as the nun asked of him, but he played like nothing even happened. He played like Grandpa never overslept, he played like Patty never over drank, and he played like the Duesenberg hadn't just crushed his little legs.

Even from behind his harmonica, Michael's smile lit up the room. He played it like he wasn't in a hospital bed, and he played it like he didn't just almost lose his life. As long as Michael still had his music, to him, he still had everything.

A little while later, Linda and Stacio got called in to speak with Michael's doctor. Dr. Bradden came into the room with a clipboard in his hands. He was a frail, old man with gray hair and bifocals. He set the clipboard down on his mahogany desk and picked up a small model skeleton.

"There's been a severe trauma to the lumbar region of Michael's spine," said Dr. Bradden, pointing around the skeleton as he spoke. "He suffered a fractured hip and a shattered pelvis. He also has paralysis in his left leg, and a slight paralysis in his right."

"Paralyzed? God, help us," Linda cried. "Our poor baby."

"What does all of this mean, Doctor?" Stacio asked.

72

"It's too early to know for sure. His right leg has a chance to function with time, but I can't promise anything."

"Will he walk again?" Stacio asked.

"I don't believe so," the Doctor said. "I'm very sorry."

Linda became hysterical. Stacio couldn't breathe. He couldn't blink, move, or cry. He couldn't do anything. He was so full of anger and guilt, he felt lost. He had no idea where they'd go from here. He couldn't draw a breath. The air had left the room. He began to panic. He had no control of himself, he wasn't sure what he was capable of anymore. His heart was overflowing with hate. He'd never felt that kind of pain in his life. Stacio didn't even recognize the voice in his head, he didn't know this man. He needed to escape. Now.

Linda reached for him, but he pulled away. "Stacio," she cried.

"I have to go," he said. "The ice, my customers, they're waiting for me."

"Stacio," Linda yelled, reaching out to grab his arm.

"I'm sorry," he said, pulling back again. "I've got to go."

He kissed Linda on the head and ran out of the hospital.

Later that day, at Degan's Icehouse, Stacio was tossing huge chunks of ice into the back of his carriage. Chestnut flinched at the sounds of them crashing onto the wooden surface. Stacio loaded the carriage like he normally did, except he threw the ice harder, and he was bare chested underneath his suspender straps. Warm breath smoked from his nostrils like a dragon in a fantasy novel. Steam danced off his shirtless body and vanished into the frozen air.

Stacio worked at a madman's pace until it caught up to him and punched him in the gut. He stumbled back and fell to his knees, exhausted. He was so helpless, it was written all over his face. You could almost feel the man's pain with your eyes. He stood back up and squeezed his fists until his knuckles cracked. He threw a melee of lightning fast punches, abusing the cold air with jabs, crosses, and uppercuts. He screamed in agony, but he didn't cry, because even if he tried to, the icehouse air was too cold to allow it.

In another burst of rage, he turned and threw a right hook that landed dead center on a massive block of ice. The shot was so fast and so powerful, the block split right down the middle. Both chunks flew off the conveyor belt and skipped across the floor. Stacio dropped his fists and stood with his head down, huffing and puffing more smoke into the frigid air. He didn't feel any pain, though.

Stacio was too numb, too numb inside and out to feel anything at all.

Chapter Nine

The Chicago Tribune

Benjamin Fitzgerald was a mess of a man, storming through the halls of the Chicago Tribune. He had darker bags under his eyes than most fifty-five year olds, and his hair was an obvious victim of neglect. Nevertheless, Ben was the editor-in-chief of one of the most successful newspapers in America. He smiled when he passed by an office that had his name on the door. He turned two more corners before making a hard left into one of the rooms. The door was wedged open with an overflowing garbage can. Ben looked down at it and shook his head. *Jesus, Max.*

Max was lounging in his chair with his feet up on the desk. He was in his early forties, and his side of the office was a complete disaster. His collared shirt was a tad-bit wrinkled, and like every other day, he wore it untucked. He never tucked in his shirt because he hated putting on a belt, and when it came to footwear, he was notorious for choosing comfort over style.

Ted sat across from him, their desks were head-to-head in the center of the room. Ted was neatly clothed, he wore an argyle vest with a bright red bowtie. Every single crease in his attire was premeditated with flawless precision. His eyes were down and his nose was buried in a thick book. Ted was ten years older, but you couldn't tell because he took so much pride in his appearance.

Ted had a motto he loved reciting to his sloppy counterpart, "The better you look, the better you feel. The better you feel, the better you write. And the better you write, the better you eat."

"Yeah, yeah, yeah," was Max's usual response. "I can write just as good in my underwear."

Ted carried and presented himself in a much more professional manner, and his side of the office was always spick and span. However, cleanliness and style aside, these were the two best writers at the Chicago Tribune.

"Maxwell, get your dirty shoes off the desk," said Ben.

"Yes, Mother," said Max, dropping his feet to the floor.

Ben leaned over with one hand on each of their desks and motioned them to huddle in close. Both men wheeled their chairs over, intrigued.

"Got a juicy tip from Precinct Nine," he said, looking back over his shoulder to make sure no one else was around. "Get this… Patty O'Banion crashed up his motorcar."

Max and Ted looked at each other and smiled. "Is the Champ all right?" Max asked.

"He's fine," said Ben, "but he hit a little boy."

Their smiles morphed into looks of concern. "Was he charged?" Ted asked. "Is the kid all right?"

"The kid's at Saint Barnabas. Apparently he's alive," said Ben. "No charges were filed. No witnesses, no police report, nothing. The whole damn thing swept right under the rug." Ben smiled, looking back and forth between Ted and Max. "So… who wants it?"

"Thanks, Fritsy, but I wouldn't touch this thing with a ten foot pole," said Max. "The people in this town worship O'Banion."

Ted thought about it for a minute. Max and Ben just stared at him. He lit his tobacco pipe and took a puff. He exhaled and shook his head. "I'd gladly expose a crooked politician or banker, people get behind that kind of thing. But going after the Champ, a celebrity like O'Banion… going after him in this town would be journalistic suicide. I appreciate you asking, Boss, but it's way too risky."

"What kind of writers are ya?" Ben flared his arms.

"Sane ones," said Max. "You know it's crazy."

Ben's face was bright red, he was frustrated and disappointed, but he knew they were right. Going after the Champ could be career suicide for either of them. The story itself would be huge for the Tribune, and the kid that O'Banion hit did deserve justice, but finding someone brave enough to investigate was going to be nearly impossible. Ben would have to find a writer with a few screws loose to take on something like this.

The thought hit Ben and Max at the exact same time. *Screwloose.*

"Give it to Screwloose," said Max. "He's nuts, and he hates Patty O'Banion with a passion."

"You just took the words right out of my mouth," said Ben, nodding his head. "Let's do it."

"Screwloose? He's still on the payroll?" asked Ted.

"Eh." Ben shrugged his shoulders. "Denny Lewis is always kind of half-on and half-off the payroll."

"He's batshit crazy, Boss, but Denny's a great writer that's never been scared of anything," said Ted. "He won't think twice about taking this on. He's your guy."

79

"And I'll guarantee he needs gambling money," said Max. "He's always about a day away from Ubano's guys busting his kneecaps."

"Either of you know where he lives?" Ben asked.

"Yeah," said Ted, "he's still at that old flop house on South Yates."

"Well, since neither of my lead writers have any balls, go give the job to him," said Ben, turning and walking toward the door. He stopped half way and looked back at Max. "Do it by the end of the day," he said, "because if we lose this story to The Chicago Sun-Times, you'll be writing obituaries for the rest of the year."

"Come on, Boss, are you serious?" he asked.

"Dead serious," said Ben.

"Excellent pun," Ted mumbled.

Max threw a crumpled piece of paper at Ted. "Come on, teacher's pet, don't egg him on."

Ted snatched the paper out of mid-air and alley-ooped it to Ben. Ben caught it and slammed it into a pile of garbage on the floor next to Max's desk. "I would highly suggest going before dark," said Ben. "It's a rough neighborhood."

He walked to the door and kicked the overstuffed garbage can back into the room. "Oh, and when you get back," he said, "clean your side of the office, Maxwell. It's disgusting." Ben slammed the door closed as he left.

"Yes, Master," said Max, tossing another crumpled sheet of paper on the floor like a spiteful child. He looked over at Ted and raised a fist. "Rock, paper, scissors," he said. "Loser goes to Denny's place."

"Absolutely not," said Ted. "He was looking right at you."

Max nodded his head in defeat. "Fine," he said, standing to grab his jacket, "but at least clean up while I'm gone."

"Absolutely not," said Ted. "My side is always spotless, and your side is always a pigpen."

"A pigpen? My side has character, Theodore."

"Character," Ted scoffed. "You're side probably has rats."

"Real nice, Ted, you've offended the rats."

The two men shared a laugh.

"Anyway, here goes nothing," said Max. "If I'm not back in an hour, call the police."

"Will do. Good luck." Ted took another puff of his pipe and went back to his book.

A few hours later, Max walked to the stoop of a rundown tenement building. The place was in bad shape. If you plucked a single stone from its structure, the entire thing would've probably crumbled. From the street, it looked one busted window away from being abandoned. It was hard for Max to believe humans actually lived there.

He was horrified, gagging and pulling his collar over his nose to mask whatever smell was festering. He moved timidly, sliding a white envelope out of his pocket. *Disgusting*, he thought, stepping over a sleeping bum. He walked through a cockroach infested hallway and slid the envelope under Denny's door. "Take the job, Screw. Get yourself out of this dump," Max whispered, tiptoeing out to avoid as much of the filth as possible.

Denny's studio apartment was even worse than the hallway. Dirty dishes, take-out containers, whiskey bottles, and crushed beer cans were scattered all over the place. It looked like a tornado ripped through a landfill and parked on his couch.

Denny groaned and covered his face as the sun snuck around the towel he had hanging up like a curtain. He peeked through his cupped hands, scanned the apartment, and spotted a whiskey bottle on the coffee table across the room. It was the only bottle he had left that wasn't completely empty. His head was pounding, probably from dehydration, but all he wanted was the hair of the dog that bit him last night.

Denny was in his mid-fifties, but he was so rough and worn out, he looked almost ten years older. He had dark, balding hair, a scruffy upper lip, and a few hours more than a five o'clock shadow. He rolled out of his messy bed and limped toward the coffee table. He stopped and clutched his head with both hands, whimpering as the throbbing in his brain intensified with every movement

When he spotted the white envelope on the carpet near his door, he changed direction. He nearly fell when he bent down to grab it, stumbling sloppily into the kitchen. He yanked one of the drawers open and pulled out a bottle of aspirin. Leaning hard on the counter, he struggled to hold himself up with an elbow as he poured four pills into his palm. He tossed the bottle back in the drawer, slammed it shut, took a deep breath, and gazed across the room at his beloved whiskey.

Denny stumbled to the couch and sat down hard. The thud shook the entire room. He popped the pills in his mouth and washed them down with his last two gulps of booze. He tore the envelope apart and unfolded the paper inside. He looked down at it, squinting and adjusting his eyes to see the fine print. Something in that letter grabbed him. He sat up straight and ruffled the paper, he leaned in close, sliding his finger over each word as he read them. "Wow," he whispered, sitting back in his seat, shocked.

After a few minutes, Denny got up and began percolating his coffee. He jumped in the shower and shaved his face. He got dressed, combed his hair, and cleaned up his apartment. He sat on a stool at the kitchen counter with a hot cup of coffee. The apartment actually looked presentable, so did Denny. He was a whole new man. He wore a shirt and tie, his hair was slicked back, and he had a pencil-sharp mustache over his lip. He looked good.

Denny put a cigarette in his mouth and picked up the letter. *Jackpot,* he thought, lighting it up and taking a long drag. He held it in for several seconds before exhaling the smoke through his nose. "Here we go, Screwloose," he said, with a devilish grin. "Here we go."

Chapter Ten

He ain't our kid

A young girl sat in front of a Steinway piano, bathing in light that poured into the grand music room through antique French doors. She reached out for the keys.

"Posture, darling," said Molly.

The young girl pulled her hands away and sat up straighter. Molly adjusted the girl's bench.

"You know that I will not accept poor posture. Knees to the edge of the piano. Back straight." Molly gently pulled the girls shoulder back. "Good, now, elbows in. Let us return to Bach, 'Air', on the G, please."

The young girl began to play, she was brilliant, a prodigy. Molly made her way to the far side of the room, she sat on a loveseat and closed her eyes with a blissful smile on her lips. She was happy with the young girl's progress. Her smile faded when she looked up and saw Patty peeking in through the French doors.

He waved her over, but Molly shook her head. She did not like to be interrupted when she was with a student. This was her home-office, and this young girl's parents were paying good money to have their daughter learn from the very best. She kept her seat and shooed Patty away.

He made a few more attempts to talk to her after her student was gone, but Molly didn't want to talk to him. Patty stood in the foyer with his fishing poles and a fully packed trunk. He was wearing a white dress shirt with suspenders, and his butler was holding out a tweed jacket. Patty slipped his arms into the jacket and checked his gold pocket watch. "She won't come down?" he asked the butler.

"She's been awfully silent, sir. Maybe a woman's issue," said the butler, shrugging his shoulders.

"Yeah, I guess so."

The butler adjusted Patty's bowtie and looked at him with a sincere expression etched on his face. "Not to pry, sir, but if it's another miscarriage, I'd just like to say that I'm deeply sorry."

That word struck an emotional nerve with Patty, but he appreciated the gesture. "No, nothing like that, Ed."

"Good, sir, I'll go get the car," he said, dragging the trunk out through the front door.

Patty nodded at him and then turned to look in the mirror. He adjusted his jacket and spun around as Molly made her way down the grand staircase. She looked like an angel, wearing a long, silk gown, with her hair pulled back, neatly as always.

"Still leaving?" she asked.

"Look, Molly, I know you're sore," he said, placing his hand on her back. "Just come to the Keys with me. It'll be nice and relaxing."

"That's impossible. I have my students."

"Please, Moll," he asked, attempting to kiss her ear. Molly pulled away from him and he didn't like it. "What do you want from me, Molly?"

"I don't want you to go, Patrick. It's not right."

"I can't cancel this trip, babe."

"It just makes me so sick, Patty, I can't comprehend it. How can you just go on a fishing trip right now? How can you enjoy yourself when we just crippled that innocent, little boy?"

"Things happen, Molly. Bad things and bad luck, they just happen."

Molly began to cry, but every time Patty reached for her she pushed him away. Patty began to pace the foyer.

"What's a stupid kid doing out so late, anyhow?" He stopped pacing for a moment and stood in front of Molly with his arms out. "What do you want… you want me to go to the parents with hat in hand? Confess? Turn myself in and beg for forgiveness?"

"Yes."

"Forget it."

"Patty, it's the right thing to do."

"It ain't gonna happen, Molly." He started pacing again, loosening his arms like he was warming up for a fight. "It ain't ever gonna happen."

Molly grabbed his shoulders and stopped him for a moment. "A child is the most amazing gift in the world, Patty. Of all people, you and I should know that. At least, I thought we should. I know it. I would do anything for a child of our own. Patty, if someone hurt our child like we hurt that boy, my God." She pulled her hands back to wipe the tears from her eyes. "This boy's mother and father have to deal with this for the rest of their lives. This is their little boy, Patty. Their baby boy."

"Listen, my grandfather watched his family starve back in

Dublin. He came here for a better life, and he got kicked around like a mangy dog." Patty grabbed Molly by the shoulders. "My father took his coal pick every single morning and crawled into that dark hole. What did he have to show for it? Two black lungs. The O'Banion name has come a bloody long way. Right or wrong, Moll."

Molly brushed his hands off of her shoulders and nodded her head.

"We don't apologize for nuttin," he said.

"But he's just a boy."

"The boy... the kid... he got a bad break is all. It happens." Patty shrugged his shoulders.

"It happens?" Molly asked, disgusted. "We broke him, Patty. We did that. Not fate or misfortune. We're responsible for what happened to him. You and I. How could you be so cruel?"

Patty smashed the mirrored wall in the foyer with one punch. "I came from nuttin," he screamed, "and now I'm the heavyweight champion of the world. Don't you forget it. I ain't sorry for nuttin. Stop being so soft, Molly, he ain't our kid. We don't have no kids."

Molly's jaw dropped, she brought her hands to her face and began to sob. Patty froze like a deer in headlights, he was instantly sorry for what he'd just said. *Shit*, he thought, *shit, shit, shit.*

They'd been trying to have children for a couple of years, but after a few miscarriages, they found out she was unable to carry to term. Patty knew that no matter how angry he was, or how bad a fight might get, he could never mention Molly's inability to give him children. It was a terribly sore and emotional subject for both of them, and she may never be able to forgive him if he slipped up.

"I'm sorry," he said. "I didn't mean... I love you, Molly. You know I didn't mean anything."

For the first time in a very long time, Patty O'Banion looked afraid. Molly just nodded her head, dried her cheeks, and forced a smile. "Have fun, dear," she said, turning toward the staircase.

"When I get back, I'll buy you that little, English sports car you wanted," he said, reaching out for her hand. She pulled away and started to walk up the stairs, cold. He pulled her hand back gently and tried to kiss it, but she slid loose and picked up her gown as she climbed the steps.

"Molly, come on."

"Lock the door on your way out," she said, never looking back.

Patty turned away and slapped himself between the eyebrows.

Stupid, stupid, stupid. He turned back toward the stairs and looked up, but Molly was already gone.

"Sorry, Moll," he whispered, before grabbing his fishing poles and walking out the front door.

Chapter Eleven

We do not fiddle

Linda was sitting in a chair next to Michael's hospital bed, she blew steam away from the spoon before feeding her son homemade, chicken noodle soup. "Your appetite is back," she said. "That's very good."

Michael nodded his head. "When can I come home, Mama?"

"Soon, dear," she said. "Very soon." Linda stood up and gathered her things. "How about lamb tomorrow?"

"With pumpkin pie?" Michael asked, smiling at his mother.

"We'll see." Linda smiled back and kissed Michael on the head before leaving the room.

A little while later, Michael was sitting all the way up in the hospital bed playing his harmonica. Molly O'Banion entered the room, she stayed quiet and out of sight as she admired his melody. Michael didn't notice her at first, his eyes were closed tight and he was lost in his music.

"Oh, Susanna," Molly said. "Good, Michael, very good indeed."

Michael stopped and opened his eyes, he set down his harmonica and studied her. "You don't look like a nun."

Molly laughed, "I'm the music teacher."

"Oh."

Molly took a few steps toward him. "Can I ask you something, Michael?"

"Yes, ma'am."

"Can you read music?"

"I think so."

"May I?" Molly pointed to an open spot on the bed.

"Sure," he said.

She sat down lightly and stared at him with loving, maternal eyes. She had to look away for a moment to fight back tears.

"Are you ok?" Michael asked.

"Yes, I'm fine," she said, clearing her throat.

"Don't be sad for me," he said, reaching out to catch a tear on her cheek. "I'll be fine."

Molly smiled. "You are an amazing young man," she said,

reaching gently for his hands to examine his fingers. "Have you ever played the piano, Michael?"

"No, but I'm saving up for a fiddle," he said, smiling. "That's why I got a job at Rudy's."

"You like the violin?"

"Yes, ma'am, I love the way it sounds," he said. "My Grandpa used to play the fiddle when he was a boy."

Molly smiled. "You know, Michael, I could teach you to play."

He stared up into her dark, almond eyes. "You really gonna teach me to fiddle? You promise?"

"No, no, no. I can promise that I'll teach you to play the classical violin. We do not fiddle, Michael," she giggled. "I'll stop by again tomorrow. How does that sound?"

"That sounds grand," he said.

Chapter Twelve

A bad mix of hate and alcohol

Linda and Stacio were standing in the kitchen, Stanley and Stevie stood in front of them at obedient attention.

"When Michael comes home, I don't want you treating him any different," said Linda.

"Yes, Mama," both boys responded.

Stacio took a deep breath and said, "He's your baby brother, but do not baby him. He will resent that. He doesn't want the attention, so don't make much of a fuss."

"Yes, Papa," both boys responded.

"If you're playing ball, you ask your brother if he wants to play," said Linda. "He can still use his arms."

Stacio cringed at that. *My boy, the cripple. My poor, little boy.* Stacio turned away as his tired eyes welled up. "You boys, go play, and remember what we told you."

"Yes, Papa," they yelled back, as they ran out the door.

"Are you all right?" Linda reached out and touched Stacio's shoulder.

"I'm fine." He placed his hand on top of hers.

Grandpa limped down the steps and sat at the table, his eyes swollen from crying. He was a devastated man, full of pain and guilt. "This is all my doing," he cried.

"No, don't do that," said Linda.

"If I would have stayed awake, he'd be fine. He would still be in one piece," said Grandpa.

Stacio was fuming inside, trying to swallow back so much rage it was drowning him. His eyes were possessed, darting around the room anxiously.

"It's not your fault, it was that cursed violin," said Linda. "If only I would have…"

Stacio erupted, flipping the kitchen table like a silver dollar. Plates and glasses crashed to the floor, forks and knives ricocheted across the room. Grandpa and Linda froze.

"Enough," Stacio screamed. "I'm the one who is accountable for the boy. I'm his father and I… I should have… I…" Stacio stopped and stormed out of the room.

Linda covered her face with both hands and began to cry. Grandpa walked over and put an arm around her. "It's all right," he said.

Linda kneeled down and started to pick up the broken glass. "I have never ever seen him like this."

Grandpa turned the table upright. "A man can only hold the weight of the world on his shoulders for so long, my dear."

Later that night, Grandpa went looking for his son in the catacomb cellar. Stacio was sitting in silence, slumped over the butcher block table with his head down. He raised his stein to Grandpa and took a gulp. Beer ran down both sides of his chin, he was clearly intoxicated.

Grandpa just nodded and walked across the room. He unlocked a cabinet and swung the door open to reveal a small arsenal. He reached inside and grabbed a revolver with a box of ammo. He popped the cylinder open and began sliding bullets into the chambers.

"What are you doing, old man?" Stacio asked.

"Old man?" Grandpa laughed. "I'm feeling pretty young with

this in my hand, and I got business to take care of."

Stacio stumbled over and grabbed his father's arm. "Pop, it's not the twenties anymore. You can't be running around with that."

"I know my way around a gun, Stacio, let me be."

They wrestled for a moment, until Stacio forced the gun down. He grabbed Grandpa by the shoulders and sat him on the empty stool. "Who do you plan on shooting this time, Pop? The tax collectors?" Stacio unloaded the bullets and put them back in the box.

Grandpa ran his hands through his hair. He took a deep breath and said, "I'm gonna kill the man that maimed your boy."

A spark ignited inside of Stacio, and that blaze was fueled with a bad mix of hate and alcohol. "What are you saying, Pop?"

"O'Banion," Grandpa cried. "Patty O'Banion ran him down on the sidewalk. He was piss drunk, and the cops let that bastard go." Grandpa wiped his tears away with both hands, clenching his fists tight. "They just left him there, Stacio. They let our Michael lie there like a stray dog. I didn't know how to tell you, son. I'm sorry."

Stacio stood up slowly, his eyes hollow, his expression blank. Anger boiled and overflowed somewhere deep inside of him, yet he felt horrifyingly calm. He set the gun down on the table and dropped the box of ammo into his empty stein. "Stay right here, Pop, I'll take care of this."

Stacio turned and stomped up the staircase. Grandpa jumped up and fumbled around with the gun cabinet, trying to get it locked. "Wait, son, the revolver," he yelled, but Stacio was already gone.

Chapter Thirteen

Elephant hunting

As usual, Patty's Place was jam packed. The music was blaring, as beautiful women swing danced with dapper men. Fedora hats, cigars, jewelry, and fur shawls were everywhere the eye could see. Kenny O'Banion stood behind the bar stuffing wads of cash into the register. Patty O'Banion was making his rounds, ensuring every customer felt special.

"Customers who feel special like to reach into their pockets," Patty always said to his brothers.

He pranced around the bar in his ivory suit, the perfect gentleman, overly gracious and thankful for their patronage. Patty finished his rounds and walked behind the bar where Kenny was working. "I love this place," he said, pouring himself a shot.

"I know you do." Kenny licked his thumb to count another stack of bills.

Richie O'Banion walked behind the bar with a wet rag and began to polish the brass tap. "Another packed house," he said.

Patty smiled and nodded, raising his shot glass. "Cheers boys," he said, throwing it back with a gulp.

"Two or three more places like this," said Kenny, "and you'll never have to jump rope again."

Patty laughed, "Peanuts, Kenny, peanuts. I should have ten places like this." He slurred a bit when he spoke. "Imagine I got Dempsey or Tunney in their youth." He threw a few punches at the air. "What a fight. Now that's a big time purse. That's a fight everyone would pay to see. There just ain't nobody else good enough no more. I'm a victim of my own success," he said, holding out his hands and smiling.

"You're a victim all right," said Kenny, "a victim of your own swollen head."

"Watch it," Patty laughed, throwing a combination of light punches in Kenny's direction.

"All right, all right, relax," Kenny said. "I'm trying to count here. Go drink some water."

Something outside caught Richie's attention and he rushed over to the blinds. "What the hell is this?"

Stacio pulled his carriage right up to the front door and jumped out. Curious patrons stopped what they were doing and began to watch. Some people moved away from the entrance, sensing trouble in the air.

"It's the Iceman," someone said.

"Never seen him out this late," said someone else.

"Richie, I thought we paid this guy off," said Kenny.

"We did."

Kenny turned toward Patty. "We owe this guy something?"

Patty wasn't scared, but he definitely seemed uneasy, totally disregarding Kenny's question.

Like talking to a brick wall, Kenny thought, shaking his head and turning back toward Richie. "Aye, just give this guy whatever he wants, and get him and his stinking horse out of here. Quick."

"I got it," said Richie, hustling toward the front door.

Stacio stormed into the bar and looked directly at Patty. Richie tried to grab him, but Stacio pushed him aside like a ragdoll, seeming far too strong for a man his size. Patty took a puff of his cigar and laughed, "Get a load of this guy."

Stacio stood out like a sore thumb in Patty's high end

establishment, surrounded by the upper class. His chest rose and fell intensely as he panted, clenching his fists with all of his might. He was still drunk, stumbling fearlessly toward the heavyweight champion.

"You," he said, pointing a finger at Patty. "You crippled my boy."

Just like that, Stacio's third enemy came to fruition. But this enemy was much more dangerous than the rest. Patty O'Banion had insane knockout power, and he came with the heavyweight title strapped around his waist.

It got quiet real fast, the swing music stopped and the entire bar was watching. You could've heard a pin hit the floor before Stacio screamed, "You were drunk! You were drunk and you crippled my boy."

A pretty woman held her hand over her mouth. "Oh my goodness," she cried.

People stirred in their seats and the entire crowd began to chatter. Everyone there looked disturbed by the accusations. Kenny was confused, glaring across the bar at his brother. *What the hell did you do this time, Patty?*

The bar began to fill with warmth, radiating through sympathetic eyes. But the only thing radiating from Patty O'Banion was narcissism, narcissism laced with a lethal dose of indifference. He didn't have a single care in the world, not for a grieving father, and not for a crippled boy whom he'd sentenced to life in a chair. Patty was actually annoyed that Stacio had the nerve to come into his establishment and ruin his night.

Patty was slumped over the bar, his eyes rolled up like a great white shark as he twisted his cigar into the ashtray. *Get over it, old man. Get over it, get the hell outta my bar, and go home to your crippled son, before I put ya in a hospital bed right next to him.* Patty was smoldering inside, standing up taller and broader as Stacio came toward him.

Kenny and Richie made eye contact, neither one of them had any idea what to do. "Patty, what the hell is this?" Kenny asked.

"Just get this pathetic drunk out of my sight," he said.

"He's crippled for life," Stacio cried. "The doctors... they say they can't fix him." He was pleading with Patty, holding his hands outward as if surrendering. "My boy... he can never become a man."

Sympathetic whispers filled the bar, while disgusted eyes stared daggers into Patty O'Banion. Anyone who wasn't looking at him gazed at Stacio with their hearts full of pity. Even Patty's brothers were touched by the Iceman's agony.

"You're my brother," said Kenny, moving in toward Patty, sincere. "Now, tell me, what did you do?"

Patty slammed his hands on the bar. "Just do what I tell ya."

Stacio looked for Patty's eyes with his hands outstretched, but Patty avoided eye contact. "Do you have anything to say to me?" Stacio begged. "Anything to say to my boy?"

Patty perked up to the crowd and smiled, looking around Stacio to see his customers. "This is just the rambling of a drunk lunatic, folks."

Stacio closed his begging hands into tight fists, his sorrow turning into fury. "You maimed my boy. Say it. Say it to everyone here," he demanded, pointed around the room.

Patty looked at Kenny with a much bigger sense of urgency. "Get this guy out of here, right now."

Stacio's haunting, blue eyes burned with fire. He leapt across the bar and threw a ferocious right hook. Patty arched back, the wild punch missing him and hitting a row of premium liquor. The glass bottles exploded one after another as they crashed to the floor.

Alcohol sprayed a woman's gown. She stumbled back, dropping red wine on a man's white suit. He flailed his arms, knocking a drink from another man's hand and onto another woman. It was a domino effect of chaos, and it spread through Patty's bar like wildfire.

Stacio wasn't a big guy, but he packed a lot of power in his punch, especially in his right hook. Maybe if Patty wasn't a professional fighter, or Stacio wasn't inebriated, that punch would've landed, and maybe the world champ would've been taking a nap behind his own bar. Unluckily for Stacio, though, he was drunk, and Patty was a professional fighter. The best of the best, as a matter of fact. So, Patty dodged the punch with ease while Kenny raced around the bar, closing in fast on Stacio's blindside.

Kenny barreled his way through the last of the crowd and whipped the Iceman in the back of the skull with his pistol. Stacio hit the floor hard, he was out cold with blood puddling around his head. Shocked guests tried to aid him, kneeling down to dab his wound with bar napkins and handkerchiefs.

Richie ran over and turned the music back on. Patty stood up on the bar and cupped his hands to his mouth, "Sorry for the spectacle, dear friends," he said. "You never know what kind of riffraff is gonna stroll through your door."

Patty jumped down from the bar, he grabbed Stacio by the arms and looked up at Kenny. "Grab his legs already."

Kenny tucked his gun away and bent down to grab Stacio by the ankles. They lifted him up and carried him toward the exit.

"One free round for everybody," Patty yelled, as they dragged Stacio through the front door. The crowd cheered as Richie started lining up glasses.

"Get this son of a bitch out of here," Patty said, spitting on Stacio as he laid face down on the sidewalk.

Kenny kneeled down and lifted Stacio over his shoulder. He tossed him in the carriage and slapped Chestnut on the rump. The horse trotted away slowly.

"You come back here and I'll kill ya," Patty yelled, walking back into the bar.

Kenny shook his head and walked in behind him. A few people were still shaken by the fiasco, but most of the bar was back on the dance floor and enjoying their free round of drinks.

"You believe the nerve of that guy?" Patty asked Richie.

"That right there was one brazen, son of a bitch," Richie said.

Kenny watched through the blinds as the carriage faded into the distance. He turned toward Patty and shook his head, wondering what kind of mess his little brother made this time. Then he walked to the bar and brushed off his suit, he looked up at Richie and held out three fingers. "Give me a triple," he said.

Richie took out a tall glass and started making his brother a drink.

"Look at this stain," said Patty, pointing at his sleeve. "Crazy old Iceman."

Kenny glared at Patty. "He didn't seem crazy to me."

"Hey, whose side you on, anyhow?" Patty asked.

"I don't know what you've done, Patty, but this is your mess. Do the right thing and clean it up before Marty finds out," said Kenny, grabbing his drink and walking to the back.

Richie chose to stay out of this one, filling three beers and delivering them to the far side of the bar. Patty just stood there, alone, deep in thought.

Denny Lewis watched Chestnut wander aimlessly down the

avenue. No one knew it, but he'd seen and heard everything that happened outside the bar. Once the coast was clear, he crept out from the shadows and limped quickly to catch up to the carriage. He hopped up and gave Chestnut's reins a gentle tug. "Whoa, horsey. That's it," he said.

When Chestnut stopped, Stacio lifted his head to look around. He had blood all over his shirt and he was still disoriented. Denny reached into his pocket and pulled out a handkerchief. He held it out in front of Stacio. "That's some gash, Iceman. Take this."

Stacio pushed his hand away and attempted to sit up.

"Easy," said Denny, "your head's bleeding awfully bad, sir."

Stacio touched his head and looked at the blood on his hand. Denny placed the handkerchief on Stacio's wound and applied pressure. "You got some enemies, huh? What's your story, friend?"

Stacio looked up at Denny. "Story?"

"Yeah, your story. Tell me why a quiet, friendly, Iceman like yourself gets tangled up with the O'Banion brothers."

"You ask a lot of questions, don't you?" Stacio grumbled, brushing Denny's hand away and pressing the handkerchief against his own head.

"You need a doctor."

"I'm fine," Stacio groaned, sitting up straight and grabbing the reins. He waved his hand out in front of Denny, presenting him with the sidewalk. Denny got the hint, he hopped down and took a step away from the carriage. Stacio whipped the reins and Chestnut trotted away.

"Thank you for the handkerchief," he said, glancing back at Denny as he rode off.

"No problem, Iceman," Denny said, cupping his hands to light a cigarette. "There's something big here," he whispered to himself. "Something real big." He smiled, inhaling a deep breath of smoke as he watched the carriage disappear into the night.

Linda was standing in her basement trying to thread a needle. She struggled to see through her tears, stopping often to dry her eyes. "Call the police, Stacio, you could have been killed."

"No," he said, seated at the table with his head bent back.

Grandpa stood over him, pouring alcohol on the gash. "You're pig headed and you never listen to me," said Grandpa. "When you go elephant hunting, Stacio, you bring your biggest gun. End of story."

"I don't need a gun," said Stacio.

Linda handed Grandpa the needle and said, "Tell him we have to call the police."

"Linda, we do not need the police," said Stacio. "That's enough about it."

"He's right, they're good for nothing," said Grandpa. "I never met a Chicago cop that wasn't on the take. Besides, O'Banion's already got Precinct Nine in his pocket. They're the ones who covered it all up."

Grandpa inserted the needle into Stacio's head. Stacio didn't even wince, he felt nothing.

Chapter Fourteen

Screwloose

Denny Lewis limped through the halls of Saint Barnabas Hospital. "Where is this kid," he muttered, peeking into each room as he passed by.

A nun turned the corner and came toward him. "Can I help you?" she asked.

Denny removed his fedora. "Thank you, Sister," he said, clearing his throat and speaking in a robotic cadence. "Where is the men's room, please?"

The nun scrunched her eyebrows and pointed him in the right direction. "Make a left here, it's all the way down on your right."

"Thank you, kindly, Sister."

Denny had never spoken to a nun before, and it showed. He did a strange bow before reaching out to shake her hand, then he pulled back and finished his bow. His eyes widened as he flashed an awkward smile. *Real smooth, Dennis.*

She looked at him funny before turning and walking away.

"Jesus, that was brutal," he mumbled, shaking his head.

He continued to peek into each room as he strolled along. He stopped in his tracks and listened closely as the sound of a harmonica played lightly through the hall. Denny tilted his head as if that would help him to listen closer. The sound was beautiful and mesmerizing, getting louder as Denny limped toward it like a bug toward a porch light. He followed the hypnotizing melody all the way to Michael's room.

He stood at the threshold and peeked inside. Michael sat alone, playing his heart out as he always did. He stopped immediately when he saw Denny's head pop into the room.

"Hey, Kid, don't stop on my account," said Denny. "I was enjoying it."

"Hello," said Michael, studying the man timidly.

"You play real swell."

"Thanks," said Michael. "It's nothing, just fooling around with my old harmonica."

Denny entered the room and sat on the foot of the bed. He dug into his pocket and pulled out a handful of gum. "Bazooka?"

"Sure." Michael lit up.

Denny handed him a few pieces before tossing a piece into his own mouth. "So, what happened to ya, Kid?"

"Motorcar hit me," Michael said, biting into the gum. "It was a real duesy."

Denny smiled and pulled a notepad from his vest. "Walking home from school, or what?"

"Leaving work," said Michael, chomping his gum. "I work at… well, I worked at Rudy's."

"That old bowling alley?"

Michael nodded his head.

"I know the place," said Denny.

"I was a pinsetter, but Grandpa called me a pin-monkey."

Denny smiled at him. "That's good. Funny," he said, scribbling in his pad. "Night job, huh? Helping out the family? I get it. A hard worker, just like your old man."

"I was saving up for something," Michael said, with a frown. "It was still there, too, right behind the glass. I just wanted to take a peek at it."

"Glass? What glass are you talking about, Kid?"

"The glass at Stroheim's store. That's where I got hit."

Denny started writing faster. "What were you looking at?"

"A violin," Michael sighed. "I only needed three more dollars. I just wanted to make sure it was still there."

"So, you were on the walkway?" Denny stopped writing and looked at Michael. "You were definitely on the walkway, Kid?"

"Yes. I swear it," said Michael. "And I just took a quick peek, honest."

"Who brought you down town?"

"I don't really know," Michael said, shrugging his shoulders.

"Maybe the police? Were the police there to help ya?" Denny pried lightly.

"I only remember a pretty woman. She was like an angel, and she smelled real nice."

"Hmm, I wonder why they sent you all the way down here."

"Beats me."

Denny handed him some more gum and stood up. "All right, get some rest and feel better," he said, patting Michael's head on his way out. "Thanks, Kid."

###

Denny strolled the sidewalk in front of Stroheim's store. He examined a missing patch of grass next to a telephone pole. He squatted down and pressed his fingers into a tire mark. Stroheim hid behind a display case and peeked out through his storefront window. Denny looked up and spotted him, but Stroheim jolted back nervously.

"Damn it," said Stroheim, smacking his forehead with his palm.

Denny ran his hands along a skid mark that led from the curb to the street. He stood up and tried to imagine the accident. He waved his hand around like a snake, and then extended his arm like an arrow, pointing his fingers directly at Stroheim's store.

Right there, he thought. *The kid was standing right there.*

Denny kneeled back down and plucked a tiny shard of glass from a crack in the sidewalk. He walked to the window and ran his fingers along it. It was squeaky clean. *Too clean.* It was brand new, standing out like a pearly white crown in a mouth full of rotten teeth.

Stroheim locked his front door and flipped his 'OPEN' sign to 'CLOSED'.

Denny shook his head and laughed, "You got nothing I don't already know, old man."

###

Later that day, Denny stood in a phonebooth crossing out numbers in a directory. He slid his finger across the page. "There," he said. "It has to be one of these two."

He reached into his pocket and pulled out his last buffalo nickel. "Eenie, meenie, miney, mo, catch O'Banion by his toe," he said, moving his finger back and forth between the last two numbers. *Here goes nothing*, he thought, sliding the nickel into the slot.

He cleared his throat, took a deep breath, and lifted the phone to his ear. He perked up and reached down deep to sound as manly as possible. "Yeah, it's the Champ," he said. "My car ready yet, or what?"

A disappointed look came over his face and he slammed the phone on the hook. "Son of a bitch," he said, shoving the door open and stepping out. "A fifty-fifty chance. I can't win with a fifty-fifty chance. You can't make this shit up," he said, shaking his head. "If it wasn't for bad luck, I'd have no luck at all."

He gathered himself and put on a friendly smile. "Anyone got a nickel? Please, it's urgent."

An old woman who was walking her dog stopped and reached

into her purse. Denny's smile widened.

The old woman scrunched her nose and said, "You all right, young man?" She thought about it for a second and then handed him the coin.

"Thanks a lot, honey buns." Denny winked at her before squeezing himself back into the phone booth.

The woman scoffed, "Damn, hobo."

A greasy mechanic was working hard under the hood of a red pick-up truck when his phone started to ring. "Son of a bitch," he said, popping up and wiping his hands on a dirty rag. He walked over to the phone on the wall and picked up, "Bo's body shop."

Denny was on the other end, speaking in a deeper voice than his own, "It's the Champ. Is she ready yet?"

"Jesus, Patty, I just got her yesterday," the mechanic said. "I told you I'm gonna need a week or two, she's pretty banged up."

Bingo. Denny hung up the phone and smiled. "Damn, I'm good."

He popped out of the phonebooth and spotted a young boy selling newspapers. "Hey, Kid, what's today's numbers?"

The kid looked down at one of the papers. "Three-four-four," he said.

"Damn it. Not a single number," said Denny. "I don't know why I even bother."

Later that night, Denny burst through the front door of the Chicago Tribune. He made his way directly to the pressroom. It was dark inside, and nearly empty. There were only a few stragglers left behind to button the place up for the night. Denny stopped in his tracks and looked around. *Where's my desk, and where the hell is Ben?*

He stormed through the room, but his old desk was nowhere to be found. Ben came out of his office and flipped off his light. He was finally on his way out, exhausted. His tie sat loose around his neck and his shirt was half way untucked.

Denny looked surprised to see him, but he wasn't half as surprised as Ben. "Well, well, well," said Ben, "look what the cat dragged in."

"Don't you ever go home, Fritsy?"

"Rarely."

"You look rough, old friend."

Ben thought for a second before he responded, "You don't.

Surprisingly," he said, rubbing his tired eyes. "The last time I saw you this cleancut, we were at the Union Daily and you were a hell of a writer." Ben stopped and studied Denny. "What do you got, Screwloose? I know that look. You got something big?"

"Something huge," said Denny. "Where's my desk?"

"Ted's got your old desk," said Ben. "I can't hold a desk for part-timers. I got my two best writers sharing an office right now. It's been tight around here with the remodel."

Denny rolled his eyes. "Listen, I need a place to work, Fritsy. Do you want the story, or do I gotta take it to Joey over at Sun-Times? I know how much you love that guy."

"Relax, Denny, you can take any desk you want," he said, waving his hand around the room, "there's nobody here."

Denny walked into Ben's office and sat behind a shiny, black Remington typewriter. He loaded a sheet of paper and scooted his chair in. He stretched his back, lit a cigarette, and started pounding on the keys. Ben sat on the edge of the desk and nodded. He was pleasantly surprised, even impressed with Denny. Denny paid him no mind, he just continued his feverish pace.

"It's good to have you back, Screw." Ben tapped Denny on the shoulder. "I guess that tip checked out?"

"Yes, sir, it did. And get this," he said, "the kid saw the car."

"Did he?"

"Yup, and he said, 'it was a real duesy'."

"A duesy?" Ben's eyebrows stretched.

"Yeah, Fritsy, a duesy. What's that fancy black convertible O'Banion loves so much?"

"Duesenberg?"

"Bingo," said Denny. "And guess who has a banged up Duesenberg in the shop."

"Patty O'Banion?"

"You bet, Frits. Patty O'Banion, Chicago's very own champ and savior."

"Listen, Denny," Ben lit a cigarette of his own and stood up, "you did good. You always do when you show up, but this thing can't be a feature. We'll bury it in the sports section. Your opinion only. The Tribune makes no accusations. Understood? Any backlash that comes from this will be coming to you. You, and you only."

"Yeah, whatever, Fritsy. I don't really give a shit. I'm playing with house money, and I got nothing to lose."

"Yeah," said Ben, "that's what I'm afraid of."

"I'm only writing the truth, Boss."

"Here's what we're gonna do." Ben paced back and forth in front of Denny. "One column in the sports section, and we'll squeeze it in this Saturday."

"Saturday? Who reads the paper on Saturday?" Denny stood up. "Fritsy, we have the elements of a Shakespearean masterpiece here. The heavyweight champion of the world runs down and cripples an innocent kid. Not to mention a police cover-up. These papers are gonna fly off the shelf."

Ben held his hand up to Denny's chest. "Tread lightly, Denny, we all know you have the subtleties of a sledge hammer. You can tie all of the coincidences together, but no accusations. Unless you find a witness from the scene of the crime, I want absolutely zero accusations. I mean it."

"Fine," said Denny. "Got five bucks?"

"I take it back," said Ben, reaching into his pocket and shaking his head.

"Take what back?"

"The part where I said it was good to have you back," he said,

The Iceman always comes on Tuesday

slamming the money on the desk and walking out of the pressroom.

Chapter Fifteen

Hush money

Marty Spiegel sat at his desk and opened up his newspaper, sipping his coffee between bites of a buttered croissant. The walls of his office were covered with boxing memorabilia and old fight posters. The biggest poster in the room was of Patty O'Banion. He was leaning on the ropes and holding the heavyweight championship belt over his head.

Marty sat up and ruffled the paper, his eyes widened as he studied what he was reading. He spit out a mouth full of coffee and slammed the paper down on the desk. The headline of the open page read, 'Precinct Nine covers up O'Banion crash'.

"He hit a kid for crying out loud. A kid," Marty screamed.

Nellie, an older man who was Marty's best friend and business partner, seemed to jump into the room. "What's up, Marty? You all right? What are you yelling about?" he asked, startled. "You trying to give me a heart attack?"

Nellie wore sweatpants and a muscle shirt. He was in good shape for his age, having been a fighter most of his life. He was a trainer now, and had trained some of the most successful fighters in the world, with Patty O'Banion leading the pack.

"Look at this," said Marty, spinning the paper around to face Nellie. He jammed his pointer finger into the heading and said, "How in the hell are we gonna clean this up? This is bad, Nell. This is real bad."

"Relax, Marty, You can't believe everything ya read."

"It's that old nut from the Tribune, Screwloose. He's crazy as all hell, but he's no hack," said Marty.

"All right," Nellie said, stroking his whiskered chin, "let's just see what Patty has to say about this before we get all upset."

"Speaking of Patty, where the hell's he been?" Marty asked. "Hiding out?"

"No, come on, Marty. He's innocent until proven otherwise." Nellie shrugged him off. "He's still promoting that bar of his. Hasn't been to the gym in weeks. Come to think of it, that's why I was coming to see you. The Champ might be getting soft on us. We gotta get him back in the gym, gotta get him training again."

"Training is the last of our worries right now. Find him and get his ass up here as soon as possible. We have serious problems."

"Sure," said Nellie, "I'm on it."

Denny 'Screwloose' Lewis had implanted a well-deserved cancer in that newspaper, and it spread fast. It infected the whole town much quicker than anyone, including Denny, thought possible. Everyone in Chicago took a bite of Denny's story with their morning coffee. The tsunami of truth hit the iron mills, the barbershops, the grocery stores, the hospitals, and the police stations. It hit everything. It lumbered through the city streets like an unstoppable force, gaining steam and sympathy for a well-loved, hard-working Iceman and his crippled boy.

"I knew it," Kenny whispered under his breath, bringing his hand to his mouth and shaking his head. He crumpled the newspaper and tossed it aside. *Damn it, Patty.*

A barber stood in front of a group of waiting customers, they were sitting on wooden chairs and listening to him intently. "Stacio's a good man, a good man with a paralyzed son. It's a crying shame."

The group shook their heads, sincere. One of the men stood up and waved his fist. "It's a damn crime, that's what it is."

An ironworker in filthy overalls stood in the center of a crowd and smacked the paper with the back of his hand. "Get a load of this crap."

The Irish police captain sprung up from his chair and tore the newspaper like an excited child on Christmas morning. "Son of a bitch," he screamed, his normally red face turning a shade of purple. "I'm gonna kill him."

Many of the doctors and nurses scattered throughout the hospital cafeteria were reading newspapers. One after another, they started pointing down in disbelief and sharing the article with the people around them. Whispers turned into a light chatter, and within seconds the entire room was in an uproar.

Ben was sitting at his desk with his feet up, he set the paper down gently on his lap. "Here we go," he said, rubbing his temples. His nervousness faded as a light smile touched his lips. "That crazy, son of a bitch," he laughed.

###

Grandpa sat comfortably in his rocker with his face buried in the newspaper. He reached out and turned the radio off. "Justice," he whispered to himself. He took a deep breath, but before he could call for Stacio, there was a knock at the door.

The dog started to bark. "Quiet," said Stacio, nudging the dog away and pulling the door open. "Can I help you?" he asked the stranger.

"Good afternoon," the man said, "Bill Drexler, attorney at law." The well-dressed man with the pointy chin and beady eyes extended his hand, but Stacio didn't shake it. He could smell bad news on this guy before he even opened his mouth. Bill pulled his hand back and placed it on top of his briefcase.

"What's your business here," Stacio asked. "I assume you didn't come for ice."

"No, thank you. I represent the interests of Mr. Patrick O'Banion and his management."

Stacio turned and looked at Linda. Without saying a word, she dropped the dish towel and took the kids out of the room. Grandpa strolled into the kitchen and leaned on the counter. Stacio took a step forward and stared into the man's eyes. "O'Banion?"

"Yes. Mr. O'Banion's acts of charity are very well known."

"Charity?" Grandpa yelled from a deeper part of the kitchen. "This guy's joking, right?"

"His management has authorized me to issue you with this one-hundred dollar check." The man smiled, pulling the check from his briefcase. "See. No strings attached," he said, shaking the check between his finger and thumb.

"A check?" Stacio tilted his head, looking around the check and directly at the lawyer.

"Yes," said Bill, "to relieve some of the medical expenses your family's been burdened with."

Stacio took another step toward Bill, leaving the man no personal space. "Where's O'Banion?" he asked, through clenched teeth. "Why isn't he here? If he had any decency, he would have come here himself. Or he would have come to the hospital. He would have apologized to our family for his wrong doing. He wouldn't have sent you."

Bill took a step back. "This visit, sir, is not personal. It's a business matter."

"Not personal?" The fire in Stacio's eyes spread. He was struggling to stay calm.

"Keep in mind, any thought of a civil suit would be very unwise," Bill said, taking another step back. "Your child was in violation of the town curfew, and no jury in Chicago would convict our beloved champion. Accept this offer, Mr. Jasinski, it's very generous."

"Beloved champion?" Stacio snapped, bull rushing the attorney. He grabbed the man by the throat and slammed him into the siding. The house shook, knocking Linda's most prized teacup from its shelf. The man shriveled with fear, grunting as his head bounced off the wood. "He crippled my son," Stacio growled, his grip tightening with each word. "Your beloved champion almost killed my boy."

Bill and Stacio both jumped at the sound of a shotgun engaging. Grandpa stormed through the front door and pressed the barrel against the attorney's cheek.

"Let me bury him, son. They'll never find his body out here." Grandpa had a crazed look in his eyes, this was far from a threat. If

Stacio gave the word, he'd already decided he was going to kill this man. "Just say the word, Stacio."

"Dear, God, please don't kill me." Bill cried, wetting his pants.

Stacio let go of his throat and pushed the shotgun barrel aside. "No, Pop, he's not worth it."

Bill cowered along the porch and down the steps, holding his throat and coughing profusely. He looked up at Stacio with blue lips and a wet crotch, petrified.

"Tell this great champion of yours to come here like a man," Stacio said, turning and walking back into the house.

"If he sends you again," said Grandpa, kicking the briefcase off the porch and scattering the man's papers around his feet, "It's your funeral. Understood?"

The attorney nodded and swallowed hard. He jammed the papers into his briefcase and ran off, never looking back.

Linda watched the entire altercation from the window with tears rolling down her face. "What a mess," she cried, sliding the curtain closed and placing her broken teacup back on the shelf.

Chapter Sixteen

Mugger McGuinn took a dive

Denny Lewis slumped over Patty's bar, looking around the room for trouble. He was completely drunk, barely able to hold up his head. He looked at one Irish relic after another, rolling his eyes and scoffing disrespectfully. He pointed to a picture of Patty behind the bar. Patty was giving a thumbs up with the heavyweight belt hung over his shoulder.

"Champion, my ass," he slurred.

A man sitting a few stools over turned to Denny, gripping his beer extra tight. "Say one more word about the Champ and I'll smack you right in the kisser."

Denny shook his head and mumbled under his breath, "Where's your champ at now? Hiding in some rat hole? Some champ he is."

The man leaned in toward Denny. "I told you to shut your fat mouth about the Champ," he said, standing up and taking his last gulp before wiping his mouth with his sleeve. "Get up, slob."

Denny turned and smiled at the man. He took a deep breath and let out a sigh, "All right."

The man raised his fists as Denny gathered himself, but before Denny was anywhere near ready to stand up, a full beer slid down the bar and stopped right in front of the angry man's stool.

"It's on the house," said Kenny, drying his hands on a little white towel. "Sit down and relax. Don't worry about this guy, Russ, we got it under control."

"All right, Kenny. Sorry about that," said Russ, sitting back down and grabbing his beer. "This maniac's driving me crazy. He's been bad mouthing the Champ all day."

"All right, all right, just ignore him. This one and the next one are on me," said Kenny, pointing to the beer in front of Russ, "then you should head out. It might get ugly in here."

"Will do, Kenny. Thank you."

"No problem," he said, pointing up at Patty as he emerged from the back. "Speak of the devil."

"Devil?" said Patty. "I'm more like a Saint."

"Yeah right," said Kenny. "That wife of yours, maybe. But you, no way."

Patty laughed, "Yeah, I guess you're right."

"Listen, this guy's begging for a beating," said Kenny, pointing back over his shoulder with a thumb. "He says you know him."

Patty leaned around Kenny to get a better look. Denny hiccupped and almost fell off of his stool.

"Jesus, this guy's a mess," said Kenny, squeezing past Patty and heading to the back. "Handle it."

"It's already handled, big brother."

Patty nodded at Russ as he walked by, stopping directly in front of Denny. Denny had his head on the bar with his eyes closed. Patty slammed down a shot glass and began to fill it. Denny lifted his head. "It's about time," he slurred.

"Denny Lewis? From the papers? They call you Screwloose," said Patty, sliding the shot in front of him. "I remember you."

"Mugger McGuinn took a dive. And everybody knows it," said Denny.

"Mugger was a bum."

"He flopped like a fish on ice. I lost fifty bucks," said Denny, waving his hands. "His damn knees buckled before you threw the punch. I saw it, I was right there… ringside."

Patty leaned in and whispered, "Maybe his knees buckled because he saw what was coming."

Denny stared up at Patty, undaunted. "How much you pay him off, O'Banion? More than those dirty cops? How much did they cost ya?"

A devilish smirk appeared on Patty's lips. "Why don't you ask them yourself?"

Denny turned around and saw the police captain with the same two young cops that were with him the night of Patty's accident. "Get up," said the captain.

"Let me finish my drink first, Officer blood pressure," Denny laughed, turning back toward the bar and reaching for his shot.

The captain slapped his hand away and the two young cops yanked him from his stool. The three dirty cops manhandled Denny through the bar, out the back door, and into the alley. The two young cops held Denny's hands on the brick wall. The captain took out his billy club and smacked it into the center of his palm as he spoke, "You'll write a retraction today. Understand? Tell the people that everything you wrote in that paper was all hogwash. All of it. Do you hear me?"

"Go to hell," said Denny.

The captain's red face almost popped. He lifted the club over his head and smashed both of Denny's hands. Denny screamed as he fell to his knees. The pain was so intense he leaned over and vomited.

"Let's see how good you write now," the captain screamed.

Denny sat back on his heels, holding out his limp hands and bawling. The captain came up behind him, grabbed a handful of his hair, and whispered in his ear, "Peck your typewriter with your nose like a chicken if you have to, I don't give a damn. I better see some good writing from you real soon, Screwball."

The captain shoved Denny's head away and kicked him in the ass. He fell forward and splashed into his own puddle of puke. The captain spit on Denny as he and the two young officers left the alley.

Chapter Seventeen

Twinkle, Twinkle, Little Star

Michael was propped up in his hospital bed, excited. Molly reached

into a box and pulled out sheets of music. "I have Mozart, Joplin, and

Tchaikovsky."

"Tchaikovsky? Is he Polish?" Michael asked.

"No, Michael, he's Russian," she said, "but that's a good guess."

A few minutes later, Michael was seated in his wheelchair,

looking much sturdier. Molly handed him a violin and took out one

of her own. "Place your fingers on the bow like this," she said,

demonstrating as she spoke. "Middle finger under your thumb. Like

so."

"Like this?" he asked, adjusting his fingers.

"Very good, Michael, here's something to start with," she said,

and began to play. "Third finger, B-flat... F... and G."

"Twinkle, Twinkle, Little Star?" he asked.

"Very good, sweetie. Now, you try."

Michael began to play, and to Molly's delight, he was a natural.

"That's it," she said, reaching out to adjust his fingers. "Not too close

to the bridge. That's it. Great job, Michael."

Chapter Eighteen

This is no taxi

Denny sat alone on his dirty couch, his hands were bandaged and his face was full of pain. He used his forearms to dig a whiskey bottle out of a brown paper bag. He held the bottle up and twisted the cap off with his mouth. "Cheers," he grumbled, tilting the bottle back on his lips.

Later, Denny sat alone again, this time at a crowded racetrack, clutching tickets in his heavily bandaged hands. He stood up and cursed to nobody in particular as three thoroughbreds raced toward the finish line. He attempted to rip the tickets with his broken fingers, but he couldn't do it. He just let them fall to the ground, hanging his head in defeat.

The next morning, Denny searched all over town for the Iceman. When he spotted him, Stacio and Chestnut were heading up Michigan Avenue. Denny took a few shortcuts through alleys and lots, trying to gain some ground. Finally, he caught up to them, limping alongside the carriage at full speed. He was in pain, panting, sweating, and struggling to keep up. "Stash," he begged, "stop, will ya?"

He reached out and grabbed for the carriage, but his bandaged hands weren't cooperating. He tried a second time, wincing as his grip slipped.

"Shit. Come on, Stash, we gotta talk."

Stacio looked at him and pulled back on Chestnut's reins. "Slow down, girl."

The carriage slowed down enough for Denny to hop on. He was out of breath and struggling to climb up until Stacio reached out and yanked him into the carriage.

"Thanks," said Denny, huffing and puffing, wiping his brow with his sleeve. "You're a strong fella."

"This is no taxi," said Stacio.

"Yeah, I know. I'm Denny Lewis from the Tribune."

"I don't need any newspapers."

"I got none to sell," Denny said, shrugging his shoulders. "I'm the writer who broke the story about your son. I'm Screwloose."

Stacio remained monotone, never taking his eyes off the road.

"What happened to your hands?" he asked.

"I got wise with O'Banion."

Stacio's jaw tightened at the sound of that name.

"You mind if I ask you a few questions, Iceman?"

"I'm not much for words."

"Yeah, I kind of got that feeling about you," Denny laughed, trying to break through Stacio's wall. Stacio's face remained hard and blank. Denny leaned in and removed his fedora. "I was in the war."

Stacio finally looked at him, scanning him in disbelief because of his age.

"Not that war," Denny said, "the first one, in 1917. I was in Belgium. Some filthy Kraut stuck me right here." Denny pointed to his thigh. "Bastard stuck me with a rusty bayonet. Damn near killed me."

Stacio didn't seem impressed. "Lucky you can still walk."

Denny reached into his hat and carefully unwrapped a medal. "It's a Silver Star," he said, holding it out to Stacio. "It represents gallantry in action against an enemy of the United States. So I've been told."

"Very nice," said Stacio, still staring straight ahead. "Thank you for your sacrifice and bravery."

"Yeah, no problem," Denny said. "Listen, Stash, I visited your son."

Stacio immediately turned toward him.

"Places like that give me the heebie-jeebies," said Denny. "I was stuck in a hospital for six years, so I try to steer clear."

"Six years for your leg?" Stacio asked.

"At first it was the leg, but they kept me in for my nerves," Denny said, seeming ashamed. "They shipped me right off to the loony bin. There were days they even jolted me with electricity for good measure. They said it could help me, cure me even. That's some way to treat a war vet, huh? Guys in the street and at the Tribune call me Screwloose because I'm a little crazy. I don't mind the nickname, but sometimes it makes it hard for people to take me seriously. This medal is serious," he said, holding up the Silver Star between his thumb and finger, "this medal was awarded to me. Awarded. Do you want to know how they awarded me, Iceman?"

"How?" Stacio asked.

"They'd just finished zapping the hell out of me, or as they liked to call it, 'my shock therapy treatment'. I was lying on the ice cold floor in a puddle of my own piss. No blanket, no water, no light, nothing. Nothing but a straight jacket and a pair of pissy briefs. They slid the medal under my door, like… like I was some kind of animal or something." Denny choked back his emotions, rubbing his eyes before tears could form. "I never got anything from anyone that really meant something to me… until this, so I kept it. It's good for a free beer here and there." Denny cleared his throat. He put his hat back on and composed himself. "I know a raw deal, mister. I do."

"I'm sorry that happened to you," said Stacio.

"It's a cruel world, my friend."

"It is."

Denny cleared his throat again and took in a deep breath. "Just trying to shoot the breeze, didn't plan to get all serious," he laughed. "So, listen, everyone's waiting for a response from your family. You ready to press charges, or what?"

"Charges? For what?" Stacio asked.

"What do you mean, for what? For justice," Denny said, waving his hands as he spoke. "Put that bum in jail where he belongs. Have you contacted a lawyer?"

"No," he said, "a lawyer will not make my boy walk again."

Denny swallowed hard and stared out toward the road, rocking with Stacio to the motion of the carriage. He looked down at his broken hands and shook his head. The two men shared a moment of peaceful silence until Denny turned toward Stacio with sincere eyes. "You're just gonna let this thing pass, aren't ya?"

"No."

"Then what are you waiting for? Money? You want a payoff, don't ya?" Denny examined the old carriage, summing up Stacio with his eyes. "I get it," he said. "The big payday. Your family certainly deserves it after what happened."

"No," said Stacio, frowning at Denny's assumptions. "I don't want his money."

Denny adjusted himself to face Stacio. "No money. No charges. What else could ya be looking for, Iceman?"

Stacio glared at Denny with a deep fire burning in his icy, blue eyes. "I want an apology for my boy."

"An apology?" Denny asked, shrugging his shoulders. "That's it?"

Stacio looked back at the road and nodded his head.

"I know it don't seem like much to ask for," said Denny, "but he ain't gonna apologize."

"He will."

"Listen, Stash, I hope he does, and he should. He should've been by Michael's bedside in that hospital begging for forgiveness. He should be begging you, your wife, and your son. He should be begging Jesus Christ, himself. He knows what he did was wrong, but he's too proud to say he's sorry." Denny looked down at his hands again, wincing as he made two fists. "The kind of man O'Banion is, I bet he ain't sorry at all. He don't care about your son. He don't care about nobody but himself." Denny took out a book of matches and put a cigarette in his mouth. He cupped his hands and lit it on the first try. He took a long puff and leaned back as he exhaled. "What are you gonna do if he won't apologize?"

Stacio pulled back on Chestnut's reins until she came to a complete stop. He bit down hard, clenching his jaw as his eyes slammed shut. He took a few deep breaths, easing the tension in his body before his eyelids sprung open. He turned his head to Denny, he looked him dead in the eye and said, "I'll beat it out of him."

Denny lit up like the giant Christmas tree at Rockefeller Center, nearly swallowing his cigarette butt. "Let me get this straight," he said, coughing and clearing his throat before leaning in close to Stacio. "Are you challenging Patty O'Banion to a fight?"

Stacio didn't hesitate for a second. "Yes," he said, "you can print that."

Denny patted Stacio on the back and almost jumped out of the carriage. "I will gladly print that for you, my friend," he said, waving goodbye with a huge smile on his face. "I'm going straight to the Tribune to take care of it today. Have a wonderful day, Iceman, and thank you for your time."

Stacio nodded and pulled away.

Denny just stood there, in shock. *An apology,* he thought. *Go figure.* "I'll beat it out of him," he laughed. "Man, oh man, what a story." Denny held up his bandaged hands, throwing punches and shuffling around the sidewalk like a boxer.

Chapter Nineteen

Pain is the only thing you'll learn here

Stacio pushed through the Grand Venetian doors and marched into Saint Anthony's Cathedral. He dipped his fingers in holy water and motioned the sign of the cross. The church was dim, with only a few worshipers sitting silently in the pews. Father Henry stood in the nearest corner, snuffing out the lowest burnt candles. He turned around and saw his brother.

"Stacio, what brings you here?" he asked, reaching out to remove Stacio's flat cap. "You know better than to wear this inside."

"I'm sorry."

Father Henry examined his head, looking closely at the stitches. "Nice job. Pop was always good with the needle."

"Take me down to the basement," said Stacio.

"For what?"

"So you can teach me. Train me like you train your fighters."

"Stacio, you're on the wrong side of the hill to be training."

"I'm strong, brother."

"What put this crazy idea in your head?" Father Henry asked.

"I'm going to fight him."

"Fight who?"

"O'Banion."

"You're gonna fight Patty O'Banion?" Father Henry laughed. "You want to fight the heavyweight champion of the world, do ya?"

"He's only a man," said Stacio, "just like you and me."

"Come. Follow me," said Father Henry, placing a hand on Stacio's shoulder.

They walked down the stairs and came into a vast basement. A regulation boxing ring sat in the center of the space, it was surrounded by heavy bags, speed bags, and other equipment. Fighters of all shapes and sizes were spread throughout the room, training and exercising. Two young fighters, wearing headgear, were in the ring sparring at half-speed.

"Keep your left up, Jimmy," Father Henry yelled across the room.

"Got it," Jimmy yelled back, muffled through his mouthpiece.

"Listen, Stacio, I understand your anger," Father Henry said. "I feel it, too. You know how much I love my nephew. However, I believe that only forgiveness will give you peace. You might not think so now, but in time, peace will come with forgiveness."

"No," said Stacio, "teach me, like when we were young. I was good once."

"You're too old now."

"You won't help me, brother?"

Father Henry lifted his hand to his brow and closed his eyes. He thought for a moment and smiled. "Stacio, pain is the only thing you'll learn here. And that pain will be excruciating for a man your age."

"I'm going to fight him," said Stacio, "with or without you."

Father Henry looked deep into his brother's eyes and knew there was no changing his mind. "Okay," he said, "let's start now."

"Good," said Stacio, walking to a table and grabbing a pair of gloves.

"What do you think you're doing?" Father Henry asked.

"Sparring."

"No, you're not," said Father Henry. "If you want me to train you, you're going to have to do exactly what I tell you. Can you do that, Stacio?"

"I can."

"Will you?" Father Henry asked.

"I will."

"Good," said Father Henry. "Put those gloves down, you're in no condition to spar."

Stacio turned around and dropped the gloves back on the table. Father Henry tossed him a smaller pair of gloves and said, "Put these on and go hit the bag. Let's see what we're working with."

Stacio, dressed in his work clothes, punched the heavy bag with ferocity. His blows were thunderous, causing the heavy bag to yank relentlessly at its chain as it flipped from left to right. After a while, he stopped to hang onto the bag and catch his breath.

"No resting," said Father Henry. "Do you think O'Banion's going to give you a hug while you rest?"

Stacio let go of the bag and lifted his fists. He was so exhausted he could barely stand.

"Again," said Father Henry.

Stacio did push-ups until he collapsed.

"Again," said Father Henry.

Stacio had his back to the wall, pulling forward on a weighted cable, screaming from the burn.

"Again," said Father Henry.

Stacio jumped rope, sweat puddling on the floor around him. He could barely lift his heavy work boots off the ground. He tripped and smacked the floor.

"Again," said Father Henry.

Stacio bear-crawled across the basement, pulling his brother on a sled loaded with cast-iron weights. He grunted and grimaced, finally collapsing at the finish line.

"Again, Stacio. Again."

Stacio could barely walk or lift his arms as he waved goodbye to his brother. He moved slowly up each step, one at a time, until he was finally out of the basement.

Father Henry stepped inside the ring and took off Jimmy's head gear. "That was brutal," he said.

"Sure was. Are you trying to kill your brother?" Jimmy asked.

"No, I'm trying to save him from O'Banion."

"No way he comes back tomorrow," said Jimmy. "Not after that."

"No way," said Father Henry. "He should be in bed for at least a week."

The next morning, Stacio limped his way into Degan's Icehouse. His body hurt so bad, he could barely stand up straight. He hobbled up to the frozen conveyor belt and started heaving blocks of ice into the back of his carriage.

Stacio pulled up to his first stop and stretched his sore muscles before reaching for his tongs. He looked up to an eighth story window and read, 'Need Ice', on a white sign with blue letters. He took a deep breath and clamped his tongs around a seventy-five pound block of ice. He marched through the entrance, found the stairwell, and labored his way straight to the top.

That night at Saint Anthony's Cathedral, Jimmy was sparring with a large man named Tickles. Tickles was in his early thirties, and he'd had his fair share of professional fights. Father Henry was in the center of the ring wearing three hats, Priest, trainer, and referee.

"Stick him with your jab, Tickles," Father Henry demanded. "Cut off the ring, Jimmy. Don't give him space."

Tickles hit Jimmy with three jabs in a row. "That's it, stick him," said Father Henry. "Nice work."

Everything came to a halt when Stacio walked in and made his way toward one of the heavy bags. Father Henry looked at Jimmy, shocked. "I can't believe it," he whispered.

"Me either," said Jimmy.

Stacio began pounding furiously on the heavy bag. Again, he wore heavy work boots with suspenders and dungarees. Stacio was shirtless this time, sporting a body that didn't hold a single ounce of fat. Despite the crow's feet starting to form in corners of his eyes, you would never think this was a man who was past his prime. His physique was flawless. Like a superhero in a comic book, Stacio was as solid as a rock.

"That's enough," said Father Henry, climbing out of the ring. "Your feet must be covered in blisters."

"I'll get used to it," said Stacio, continuing to pound the bag.

"Come on. Stop," said Father Henry, grabbing him by the arm. "Come in the back. I have the proper gear for you."

"I've worn work boots every day of my life. Thank you, but I'll wear what I have."

"Fine, do you still want to spar?" Father Henry asked.

"I do."

"Hop inside," said Father Henry, motioning his hand toward the ring, "if you think you're ready."

"I am."

"We'll see about that."

Stacio stood in his corner of the ring, stretching out and slamming his gloves together. Father Henry was in the opposing corner, standing in front of Tickles. He fed the big man his mouthpiece and looked him straight in the eyes. "Pummel him," he said. "Do you understand me?"

"You sure?" Tickles asked. "That's your brother."

"Destroy him, Tickles. The quicker he gives up on this O'Banion business, the better off he'll be," said Father Henry. "It's for his own good."

"All right, Father. Will do."

Father Henry jumped down and rang the bell. Stacio and Tickles shuffled to the center of the ring and touched gloves. Stacio didn't move much. He held his hands up around his head, glaring across the ring at his opponent. Tickles circled him, bobbing and weaving, firing quick jabs into Stacio's face.

"Keep your hands up, Stash," Father Henry yelled into the ring.

"Tighten that guard."

Tickles kept firing jabs. Left. Left. Left. Stacio just absorbed each blow, never attempting to counter. Tickles landed close to twenty left jabs before the bell finally rang. Stacio turned and walked to his corner, his face was covered in welts. He refused his water and his stool, opting to stand up and wait for the next round to begin.

"Throw your right cross and put him on his backside," said Father Henry, making a tight fist with his right hand. "Finish it."

"All right," said Tickles, standing from his stool. "I'll finish it."

The bell rang and both men rushed the center of the ring. Tickles jabbed again. Left. Left. Left. Stacio took each blow, unfazed. Tickles swooped in again with more jabs. Left. Left. Left. After the third jab landed, Tickles set his feet and loaded up his right cross. Boom! It landed perfectly on Stacio's chin. He stumbled backward, but instantly regained his composure.

Just like that, a fire erupted in Stacio's eyes. He tilted his head and stared a hole through the big man. Tickles quivered, unable to believe Stacio was still standing after a shot like that. *This guy's tough,* he thought, his confidence morphing into fear as he found himself frightened by the much smaller man.

Stacio stomped forward, bobbing and weaving, but still not throwing punches. Tickles back peddled in a panic, throwing sloppy defensive jabs. Stacio pounced on one of the jabs, countering with a right hook to the ribs. Boom! Tickles keeled over, wailing and clutching his side with both gloves. At the speed of lightning, Stacio pulled his right glove out of the man's body and hit him with another powerful right hook to the head.

His mouthpiece launched out of the ring and bounced onto Father Henry's shoe. Tickles took flight, both of his feet leaving the ground for a moment. He was asleep in mid-air, almost collapsing the ring when his stiff body smacked the canvas. Tickles was down for the count, he may have slept through the night if they let him. Stacio dropped his hands, looked down at his brother, and said, "I'm ready."

Father Henry looked shocked. Jimmy looked shocked. Every single person in the basement looked shocked.

"Two punches. Are you kidding me?" Jimmy laughed. "We got us a fighter."

"Back up," Father Henry yelled, climbing into the ring. "Go back to your corner, Stacio."

Father Henry knelt down next to Tickles and removed his head gear. "Are you okay, Son?"

Tickles lifted his head from the mat, he was disoriented. "Lucky punch," he said, trying to get up. He struggled for a moment before giving up and lying back down. "Ugh, I feel like I got hit by a truck, Father."

"Yeah," Jimmy whispered, nudging the guy next to him, "an ice truck."

Father Henry looked over at Stacio, who was pacing back and forth in his corner like a caged animal. He showed no emotion at all, no remorse, no pride, no excitement. Just pure focus. Father Henry examined his brother and grinned. "That was no lucky punch," he said, standing up with his hands on his hips. "We're gonna need more sparring partners."

Chapter Twenty

Iceman challenges the Champ

Marty barged through the front door of Patty's Pace. It was early and nobody was there except Patty, throwing darts and drinking alone. "Whoa, Marty, easy with the door," he said.

Marty walked up to Patty and slammed a newspaper down on the table. "Did you see this absurd headline?" Marty asked, jabbing his finger down on each word as he read them, "Iceman challenges the Champ."

Patty rolled his eyes and threw another dart. "It's hogwash, Marty. Don't worry about that."

"Why's the Tribune keep giving this lunatic space?" Marty asked. "I thought you said you took care of this Screwloose character."

"Don't get all excited," said Patty, holding his palm up to Marty. "Everything's fine, this guy's just a shell-shocked drunk."

"A shell-shocked drunk that can write his ass off," said Marty.

"People keep reading this kind of stuff and they'll turn on you. They'll turn on us." Marty started pacing the room and taking deep breaths. "This guy's good, Patty, we got us a Goddam Mark Twain on our hands."

"No one reads that bum's opinion. Trust me," said Patty. "He's just a broken down, degenerate gambler."

"I dunno." Marty stopped pacing and grabbed his hair with both hands. "I heard two gardeners talking about it this morning. Everybody's talking. This Polak Iceman's calculating something. He's playing us, Patty, I know it."

Patty walked behind the bar and poured himself another drink. "It's nuttin, Marty, relax. He's just looking for a bigger payday," said Patty, "and now, he ain't gettin nuttin. I ain't worried about it, besides, we got the cops on our side."

"Just stay away from this Iceman," said Marty. "Crazy people make me nervous, Patty, you never know what they'll pull."

"I ain't scared of nobody," Patty snapped, slamming his drink on the bar. "If he comes back in here, I'll knock him through a wall. I'll put that Polak in a hospital bed right alongside that boy of his. Kid should've been home sleeping, anyhow. I'm sick of talking about it."

"Jesus, Patty," Marty mumbled under his breath. He closed his eyes and began massaging his temples. "What am I gonna do with you?"

Linda was lying in bed, she was perched up on her elbow with a hand pressed to her cheek, looking across the room at her husband. Stacio groaned and climbed into bed slowly. Aches and pains made his motions choppy as he leaned in and tried to kiss her goodnight. Seeing him struggle, Linda leaned in the rest of the way and gave him a kiss.

"Why are you doing this to yourself, Stacio?"

He laid back slowly and let out a sigh of relief. He ignored her question and stared up at the ceiling.

"I don't want you to get hurt," she said. "I couldn't bear it."

"I have no choice," he said.

"You always have a choice, Stacio."

"We were robbed, Linda. Our Michael was robbed. You must understand why I have to do this," he said. "I'm doing it for him, just like I would do it for any of our sons. And just like I would do it for you. A man must protect his family, Linda, and I will protect mine."

"You are a great man, Stacio, but this… this is killing you."

"No, it's making me stronger," he said. "Besides, I'd rather die than let him get away with what he did to Michael."

"I understand," she said, laying her head down and putting a hand on his chest. "I'll just keep praying for you, then. Goodnight, dear."

"Goodnight, Linda," said Stacio, kissing her hand before resting his tired eyes.

Chapter Twenty-one

Confession

Stacio was back at it, pounding viciously on the heavy bag. He swung his fists with angry intentions. Father Henry was barely able to hold the bag, getting tossed around the room like a ragdoll. The power behind each punch was incredible.

"Stop. Stop. Stop," Father Henry pleaded, almost losing his footing.

Stacio dropped his hands and walked away to catch his breath.

"You must think," said Father Henry, "if you don't bob and weave, a skilled fighter will use your aggression against you. You'll be a sitting duck for O'Banion. He'll take you apart if you sit still for even a second."

Stacio nodded. "Again, then," he said, walking back to the heavy bag and continuing his onslaught.

"Enough," said Father Henry, placing a hand on his brother's shoulder. "It's time. I want you to come upstairs with me."

Father Henry led Stacio upstairs to the confession booths.

"What is this?" Stacio asked.

"You have to confess what's on your heart," said Father Henry. "It will only help you."

"I won't do it," said Stacio. "You're my brother, it doesn't seem right."

Father Henry grabbed Stacio and pushed him inside. "Brother or no brother, I'm your trainer," he said. "And this is a very important part of your training. You need this."

Stacio sat inside, rubbing his sore hands. He lifted his head as a small door slid open between them.

Father Henry's voice spoke softly, "Confess your sins, brother."

Stacio looked down at the floor. "I... I don't know what to say."

"Have you ever lusted for another woman?" Father Henry asked.

"Lusted?" Stacio asked. "No, I have not."

"But you have fancied another woman, haven't you?"

Stacio thought for a moment before he spoke, "There was a customer I was very fond of. Francis."

"Did you find her beautiful?" he asked.

"She was very beautiful," said Stacio.

"Did you crave her?"

"No," said Stacio, "I cared for her more like a sister."

Father Henry nodded his head and smiled. "You sell ice for a living."

"I do."

"Times have been tough," said Father Henry. "Have you ever cheated anyone?"

"No," said Stacio, offended. "Never."

"There's bitterness inside of you, Stacio. Tell me about that."

Stacio took a deep breath and said, "Michael was innocent."

"No, Stacio, this anger has been simmering long before Michael's accident," said Father Henry. "You think you can take on this evil world all by yourself. You think you can right all of its wrongs. You fight tooth-and-nail, brother. You fight to right them to your own ideals, but that is not the way. The weight of this world on one man's shoulders will always crush him in the end. The world is always changing, Stacio, even if it's not for the best. You must adapt to it, not the other way around. You can't keep fighting it, because it's a fight no man can ever win."

"This is true, brother, I do live in a time that has passed," Stacio said. "Old ways, old traditions, a simpler life. I can't help the fact that I was born a century too late. There is no conforming for me, it's just who I am. It's who I've always been."

"I know it is," said Father Henry, "but if you don't conform to time, Stacio, then time will leave you behind."

Stacio didn't respond, he just closed his eyes and rubbed his hands.

"This is the world we live in now," said Father Henry. "The police are corrupt, the politicians, even the clergy. You can't change it, brother, nobody can."

"I can try," said Stacio. "A man can always fight for what he believes in."

Father Henry sat up and turned toward the small opening. "You're throwing punches at ghosts," he said. "You're swinging at the stench in the air like a madman, only to have that same stench suffocate you before you can catch your breath. It's foolish, Stacio. You can't right the wrongs of this world on your own. This is a cold fact."

"Am I to do nothing?" Stacio asked. "I would fight fifty world champions at the same time before I let something like this go unpunished."

"That's understandable," said Father Henry, "but you must still forgive. For this, and for everything else. Forgiveness is your only salvation, Stacio. Forgiveness is the only thing that can settle your soul."

"You've seen my son," said Stacio. "You've seen Michael in that bed, mangled by O'Banion." He paused, looking hard through the screen, trying to locate his brother's eyes. "Have you forgiven, Father? Have you truly forgiven the man that did this to Michael?"

The two men shared a long moment of silence. Father Henry finally looked up and shook his head. "No," he admitted, "I have not."

"I'll confront him again," said Stacio, "but this time I'll be sober. I know he's a large man and a strong man. He's the heavyweight champion of the world for good reason. He may be able to crush my skull with his bare hands, I don't know." Stacio's eyes were intense as he spoke. "But I'm not scared, brother. There is no fear inside of me."

"I know there isn't, Stacio, that's what scares me."

"Is my confession over?" he asked.

"Yes," said Father Henry. "You may exit."

Both men stood up and came out of their booths. Father Henry had a smile on his face, a mixture of fear and excitement. "I just wanted to see where your heart was," he said. "If you really want this fight, so be it."

"What if he refuses to fight me?" Stacio asked.

Father Henry laughed, "No Irishman's ever turned down a fight."

Chapter Twenty-two

Amazing Grace

Grandpa was napping comfortably in his rocker. Linda heard light chatter coming from the radio when she walked into the livingroom and nudged him.

"What is it?" he asked.

"Come on, we gotta get this out of here," she said, helping Grandpa up before grabbing one end of the radio. "Grab your side."

Grandpa limped over and wiped the sleep from his eyes. "Where are we taking her?"

"To the family room. Michael's coming home soon and this is where he'll sleep."

"All right, but be careful," he said, shuffling his feet slowly, "these old tubes are fickle."

###

A few weeks later, Michael was sitting in his wheelchair at the kitchen table, carving pumpkins with his brothers. Linda smiled at

him from the stove as she stirred a pot of soup. Michael looked up at

her and smiled back, he was happy to be home.

Later, he wheeled himself to the window and peeked out through

the lace curtains. His brothers were outside tossing a football around

the yard. The boys stopped playing when a black Lincoln

Continental turned onto their road. The family dog gave chase,

jumping and barking at the Lincoln's tail lights.

Molly sat in the passenger seat as Edward, the butler, drove

slowly up the dusty driveway. Ed was wearing a leather chauffeur

cap and a silk apricot scarf. He smiled at Molly as he stopped and

pulled up on the emergency brake. "Here we are, Ma'am."

"Here we are," she repeated slowly, stepping out of the car and

admiring the property. "Hello, boys," she said, waving at Stanley and

Stevie, who were leaning on a large maple tree across the yard.

The boys waved back, hypnotized, gawking at this beautiful

woman in her black sable. Ed peeked up at the old farmhouse and

gave a look of disdain at the boys in their beat up dungarees. "Are

you sure that you want to be involved with these rubes, Ma'am?"

"These people are fine, Ed."

"Very well," he said. "Shall I carry in your things?"

"No, thank you. I'll send these young men to fetch them."

"I'd prefer that I accompany you, Ma'am."

Molly took a deep breath. "Thank you, Ed, but I'll be fine."

"As you wish," he said. "I'll be right here waiting for you."

"Thank you. Wish me luck."

"Good luck, Ma'am."

Inside, the doorbell rang throughout the foyer.

"Coming." Linda wiped her hands on her apron and answered the front door. Molly stood across from her, looking stunning, she was as elegant as a Hollywood starlet.

"Hello," said Linda, confused. "How can I help you?"

Molly boldly entered the house, carrying a packed violin case. She looked around, smiling as her eyes came back to Linda. "I'm Miss Molly," she said, stern, but friendly. "I'm Michael's music teacher."

"Oh." Linda scrunched her eyebrows.

Michael wheeled into the foyer and lit up when he saw her. "Miss Molly," he yelled.

Stanley and Stevie came running in behind her, curious, but

mostly just enchanted by her beauty. They both stared at her with delight.

"Who hired you?" Linda asked.

"I only have an hour, we must get started," said Molly, very direct. "Hello, boys, you look nice and strong," she said, pointing to the door. "I have two boxes in my car. Ed will show you to them. Please bring them in quickly."

"Yes, ma'am," said Stanley, running out of the house with Stevie on his heels.

"Very good manners," said Molly, smiling as she touched Linda on the shoulder.

"Thank you," Linda said, smiling back. "Would you like some coffee?"

"No, thank you," said Molly. "We must begin promptly."

Stanley and Stevie returned with her boxes.

"Set them down right here, please," she said, pointing into the living room. "Thank you, boys."

"You're welcome, Ma'am," the boys replied in unison.

Molly wheeled Michael into the living room. "No interruptions for sixty minutes, please," she said, before sliding the pocket doors closed. "Thank you."

Within seconds, Michael began to play the violin.

Linda turned to Grandpa, she pointed to the door with her thumb and whispered, "Is that Michael playing? When did he learn to play the violin?"

"Michael's one of them fast learners," said Grandpa. "She must be one of them fast teachers."

"I guess so." Linda shrugged her shoulders.

"Either way," said Grandpa, "I like her."

"Me too," said Stanley, with hearts in his eyes.

"Me three," Stevie said, blushing.

"My goodness," said Linda, placing one hand on each of her sons and guiding them toward the door. "Go play."

"Good golly, Miss Molly. Huh?" said Grandpa, bouncing his eyebrows and nudging them with an elbow as they passed.

Both boys laughed as their cheeks turned red.

"Shush," said Linda, widening her eyes and clenching her jaw at Grandpa.

Stanley and Stevie giggled as they ran out of the house. Grandpa laughed along, waving to them as they left. He looked up at Linda with a mischievous smile. "I couldn't help myself."

Once the boys were out of sight, her serious expression faded. She shook her head at Grandpa and laughed, "Jeez, Louise, you're terrible."

Molly sat on the edge of her seat, her legs were crossed and her posture was perfect. Michael was sitting in front of her. He placed his bow down and laid the violin across his lap.

"What is rule number one?" she asked.

"Tune the strings?"

"That's right, Michael, every single day," she said. "Gut strings are very unpredictable."

"Tune the strings every day," he said. "Got it."

"Now, what is rule number two?"

"The sticky stuff?" he asked.

"Yes, the rosin," said Molly. "Except this time we apply it to the bow and not all over your little fingers."

Michael grabbed the bow and began to stroke it across the rosin. "Smells funny," he said, crinkling his nose.

"Yes, it's made of pine sap."

Michael looked up at her and smiled. "You sure are awfully

smart."

Molly smiled back. "Well, thank you, Michael."

"You're welcome."

"Is the instrument ready?" she asked.

"Yes, ma'am," he said, tucking the violin under his chin.

Molly leaned back in her seat to get more comfortable. "Begin."

Michael grabbed his bow and slid it lightly over the strings.

"Good, now, adjust your pitch," she said, tapping her foot to the rhythm. Molly closed her eyes tight and focused on the music. "Relax your fingers, Michael. Do not put weight on the strings until you're ready."

Michael took a deep breath and began playing 'Amazing Grace'.

"Beautiful," she said. "Excellent vibrato, Michael."

Molly opened her eyes and smiled with delight. She leaned over and removed another violin from one of the boxes. She gave the bow a few slides over the rosin before she joined in. Then, they played together in perfect harmony for nearly sixty minutes.

Linda turned from the kitchen sink and looked at Grandpa. "Do you hear him in there? I can't believe he's playing the violin like that."

"That kid could pick up anything and play it," said Grandpa. "He's got a real gift for music."

"It's hard to believe, but he seems happier than ever," said Linda.

"He sure does," said Grandpa.

Linda smiled and tossed her dish towel over her shoulder. She walked across the room and kissed Grandpa on the forehead. "Thank you, Pop."

He looked up at her, confused. "I'd never complain about a pretty girl planting a kiss on me," he said, "but what are you thanking me for?"

"For her," she said, pointing toward the door. "Miss Molly had to be your doing."

Grandpa shook his head and said, "It wasn't me."

Linda nodded, pursing her lips and studying him. Trying to get a read on Grandpa was a tough job, he had an unshakable poker face. However, the process of elimination left Grandpa as the only possible choice. *You're pretty good, old man, but I know it was you.*

"So, she just came down from the heavens?" Linda asked, with a smile.

Grandpa bounced his eyebrows and laughed, "She sure is the

cat's meow."

Linda smacked him with the dish towel. "Don't be rude, old man."

Chapter Twenty-three

My family, my fight

Sunday morning at Saint Anthony's Cathedral, Father Henry spoke out to a jam packed church. Sunday mornings always brought in a good sized crowd, but that day the crowd was more than double its normal size. The pews were overflowing and there was barely any standing room. It was by far the largest crowd Father Henry had ever drawn to Saint Anthony's.

The energy inside the church had the same feel as Christmas Eve or Easter Sunday, where people who only went to church two times a year would show up like it was mandatory, overly focused and ready to listen to every single word the priest had to say.

All of the Sunday regulars were in attendance, but most of the congregation was made up of newcomers. Newcomers who were drawn to a church in support of the small Polish boy that had been brutalized by the world champ. An innocent child who'd been wrongfully treated by the law, and forgotten all together by justice. A small, helpless boy whose father - only half the size and nearly double the age of the heavyweight champion – was willing to risk his life to avenge his son.

Almost every family in the church was of the working class. The women wore simple dresses, and the hard, scruffy men had calluses on their hands and work boots on their feet. They didn't come to Saint Anthony's just for Sunday morning worship. These people came to support the Iceman, they came to join in the fight against Patty O'Banion. They came to be part of something they believed in, something that would go down in history.

Father Henry stepped up to his podium, he took a deep breath and began to preach, "When a young, innocent child is struck like this, treated like this, a mindless act of irresponsibility becomes an act of sheer cruelty. Being drunk and running over a precious child may have been an accident, but leaving that little boy in the dirt to suffer while they planned out their cover-up, that was fully intentional. This kind of inhuman behavior is unacceptable, and something must be done. We must stand together. Every last one of us," he said, commanding the stage like a four-star General. "Yes, it's true, Jesus teaches us that we should turn the other cheek, that we should find it in our hearts to forgive." Father Henry gripped both sides of the podium with his jaw clenched. He squeezed until his knuckles turned white. The entire congregation tensed when he paused, all eyes locked on the Priest. Nobody in the church would blink or breathe until he spoke again. "But not this time," he said, lifting his fiery eyes to the crowd. "As guardians of these children, as protectors of these innocent children, we must be vigilant. This helpless child needs a voice, and I will be that voice. You will be that voice, this entire congregation will be that voice, and we will not stop until we are heard!"

The men began to stir in their pews, grunting and nodding in agreement.

"Justice must prevail," Father Henry continued, waving a hand over the crowd. "Mill workers, carpenters, barbers, gardeners, everyone… we must all strike… all of us… together. We will never ever turn the other cheek to this. Not when it comes to our families, and not when it comes to our children. We are fighters by nature, and we will always fight to protect our own."

The church erupted. All of the men stood up from their pews, hooting and hollering. The nervous women tried to pull their husbands down, but it was no use. This motley congregation was fired up and ready for war. Father Henry looked on in awe. He nodded his head in approval as a smile formed on his lips.

Later that cold, autumn morning, Father Henry came around the side of his brother's farmhouse. He followed the sound of grunting and smashing. When he peaked around to the back, Stacio was chopping wood. He was shirtless, wearing only boots, jeans, and suspenders.

Father Henry was amazed, watching his brother's warm breath smoke into the chilled air. "Nippy morning," he said, catching Stacio's attention, "for us humans, anyway."

Stacio smiled, swinging his ax and splitting a thick log with a single blow.

Father Henry shivered in his wool coat and hat, tightening the scarf around his neck. "You're unbelievable, brother, it's freezing out here," he said, blowing into his hands. "The cold never bothered you a bit."

"No," said Stacio, "I never really feel cold."

Father Henry studied him for a moment. "You know, I remember mother saying that when you were a baby she had to bring you out on the cold porch to get you to sleep sometimes. You've always been that way. You really were born to be an Iceman."

"Stanley says I have penguin blood." Stacio smiled.

Father Henry laughed, "Penguin blood? That's good," he said, "I like that."

Stacio stopped smiling and looked at his brother with a serious expression.

"What is it?" Father Henry asked.

"It's time to go see him. I'm ready."

"You'll need my help."

"No," said Stacio, "I'll go alone. This is my family, my fight."

"Very well, brother. Just be safe."

Chapter Twenty-four

Rabid congregation

Denny Lewis limped out of a barbershop on Sunday afternoon in Uptown Chicago. He wasn't three steps from the exit before two thugs grabbed him.

"You have Ubano's money?" the larger thug asked.

"He'll get it next week," said Denny, breaking loose and straightening out his collar. "Look, I'm working again, fellas." He held out a newspaper.

"Who lumped up your hands?" the smaller thug asked.

"Cops," said Denny.

"Well, veteran or not," the larger thug said, looking back over his shoulder as they walked away, "you better pay next week or I gotta put your knees over a cinder block. Capiche?"

"I always pay," said Denny, "you guys know that."

Denny turned and walked in the opposite direction. He stopped in front of a fruit vendor and grabbed a peach. "Hey, Mur, the peaches are hard as a rock."

"Yeah, Screw, just like your head," said Murray. "Hey, I saw your guy a minute ago."

"Who'd ya see, Ubano?" Denny asked.

"No, the Iceman," Murray said. "He just went up Michigan Ave."

Denny dropped the peach and jumped in a cab. "Up Michigan until we catch the Iceman," he said. "You can't miss him, he's in a horse and buggy thing."

"Yeah, I know Stacio," the driver interrupted. "I just saw him."

"Good. Find him and cut him off, please. And step on it."

Stacio pulled Chestnut's reins when the checkered cab cut him off and jammed on its brakes. Denny hopped out, threw money at the driver, and limped toward Stacio with his hands up. "Iceman, please don't move," he begged, bringing his hands together in prayer, "I'm too old to be chasin' horses."

"You again," Stacio said, motioning to the empty seat beside him. "Come, then, I'm in a hurry."

Denny smiled and climbed up. "A little late for an ice delivery, don't ya think?"

"I have no ice."

"So, what are you going up Michigan for?"

"I have something to settle," Stacio said.

"Going to Patty's joint, huh?"

"Yes."

Denny was excited at first, reaching for his pad with a huge smile on his face. He knew that whatever the outcome of that visit to Patty's Place, the story was gonna be huge. It would sell lots of papers, it would have his name all over it, and he literally had a front row seat to the action.

But Denny's smile faded as he took a hard look at the Iceman. He could feel the pain radiating from Stacio's heart, and he didn't like it one bit. *These are real people. Good people*, he thought, *and this little boy's never gonna get out of his wheelchair. It's sad stuff... unfair stuff.* Denny sighed and shook his head, but said nothing.

He just frowned as he looked down at his aching fists, reflecting back on his bandages and how they came to be. He turned to Stacio for a moment, the two men rocking peacefully again to the motion of the carriage.

"Don't do it, Iceman," Denny pleaded, "it's a bad idea."

Stacio paid him no mind, keeping his gaze locked straight ahead.

He was a man on a mission, there was no use in trying to change his mind, but Denny was a gambling man who wouldn't be able to live with himself if he didn't give it a shot.

"Look at this. Look at my hands," said Denny, waving his palms in front of Stacio. "This plan you got in your head is madness. He's got dirty cops on his payroll. You probably won't even get in the door. Even if you do make it inside, you won't get nowhere near O'Banion, I guarantee you that."

"We'll see," said Stacio, stopping Chestnut directly in front of Patty's Place.

There was a small crowd outside standing in front of the entrance. Everyone tensed up as the carriage stopped.

"Oh no, it's the Iceman," someone said.

"Yup," another person confirmed, "that's him, all right."

Stacio stepped down from the carriage, tugging his cap tight to his head as he scanned the crowd. Nobody had anything to say, they just scattered and waited to see what he was going to do. Before Stacio entered the bar, he turned back to Denny, "Could you do me a favor?" he asked.

"Sure can," said Denny, "what is it?"

"Make sure no one spooks her," said Stacio, patting Chestnut's mane.

Denny grabbed onto her reins. "Not a problem, Iceman. Good luck in there."

Stacio nodded to Denny, then he turned around and marched into the overcrowded bar. A path formed in front of him, splitting farther through the congestion with each step he took. When the alley finished forming, Stacio stood at one end and the O'Banion brothers stood at the other. Patty looked up from the cash register, he had Kenny to his left and Richie to his right. All three of them spotted Stacio at the same time.

"Oh, shit," Kenny said, and the whole place went silent.

Patty and Stacio locked eyes. Patty almost cringed at the smaller man's fearlessness.

The Iceman took another step forward and cleared his throat. "They say you haven't been fighting because the contenders are afraid to get into the ring with you," he said, staring a hole through the Champ. "You don't scare me, O'Banion. I want to fight you."

The crowd gasped, and nervous whispers infested the room. The police captain took his last gulp of beer and slammed his mug down on the bar. He stood up and wiped his sleeve across his mouth. "I'll take care of this lunatic," he said.

Patty reached over the bar and placed a hand on the captain's shoulder. "Sit," he said, "I got it."

For a brief moment Patty felt an ounce of pity for the broken father. "Look, Iceman, I ain't got no beef with you."

"You crippled my son," Stacio shot back.

The crowd began to stir. Whispers turned into chatter and people were becoming uneasy.

"Do you have anything to tell me?" Stacio asked.

A few of the patrons seemed sympathetic toward Stacio. Some of them were upset with Patty, but most of them were angry that the Iceman came back into their territory looking for trouble. There was a clear split, with vast confusion over what really happened and who was right or wrong.

Patty was nervous that his clean name could be in jeopardy, but he was more annoyed than anything, and that annoyance was written all over his face. He had no intentions of apologizing, and he was all out of patience. He took a deep breath and tried to calm himself down. All he wanted was for the Iceman to disappear and the whole thing to be over, but he knew that Stacio was never going to quit.

Patty's blood pressure skyrocketed, redness traveled up his neck and flushed his cheeks. He didn't care anymore, he was done trying to portray the good guy. Patty leaned on the bar and began to scream, "Yeah, I got something to say." Spit shot from his mouth with every word. "Don't let your kids out in the middle of the night. Now, scram, old guy, before you get yourself hurt again."

Stacio kept his eyes locked on Patty. Unafraid, he stomped deeper into the alley and removed his jacket.

"This guy's nuts," said Richie.

"No," said the police captain, turning toward Stacio and slapping his billy club into his palm, "he's just a thick-headed dog that needs to learn his place."

Stacio took two quick steps toward the police captain and stood chest to chest with him. "You're the one who left my boy on the sidewalk, aren't you?" Stacio almost growled as he spoke.

The captain grinded his teeth. "Step back, Pole," he said, jabbing the billy club into Stacio's chest, "or else."

Stacio stood his ground, unfazed.

"Have it your way," the captain said, "filthy, Polak."

He cocked his billy club back and swung for the fences. Before the club hit Stacio, Father Henry came out of nowhere and grabbed the captain's wrist. The two men began to wrestle back and forth for the club.

"Relax, Father," said Patty, "this ain't got nuttin to do with you."

"Repentance," said Father Henry, locking his eyes on Patty while still trying to wrestle the billy club away from the captain, "ask for our family's forgiveness and you shall receive it."

Furious, Patty glared at Stacio, then back at Father Henry. "It'll be a cold day in hell, Priest."

Outside, Denny held tight to Chestnut's reins, watching dozens of Father Henry's rabid congregation force their way into the bar. "Jesus," Denny mumbled, "you seeing this, horsey?"

As more of Father Henry's followers crammed inside, the crowd became agitated. It swayed from left to right, tossing people around and knocking drinks to the floor. As the crowd swayed hard, the billy club slipped and smacked Father Henry on the top of the head. He fell to the floor with his hands over his face.

"Father," a young man yelled.

"They hit Father Henry," an older man screamed.

"He's hurt," said a third man.

The captain lifted his billy club again, but before he could swing it, Stacio shot at him like a bullet. The Iceman threw a right hook that landed directly on the captain's chin, putting him to sleep before his fat body slapped the floor. He went down like a ton of bricks, and it was a long time before he got up again.

Every man from Saint Anthony's Cathedral seemed to be inside Patty's bar, and not a single one of them was there to 'Have a drink with The Champ'. Two men trampled all over the captain's head and chest trying to get to Father Henry. They yanked him up to his feet and got him away from the commotion. The angry mob stormed through the bar like bulls in a china shop. Within seconds, Patty's grand piano was flipped upside down with all four legs busted off.

"My bar," Patty cried, "not my bar."

Kenny and Richie tried to protect him, keeping him restrained while dragging him toward the back.

Tables, chairs, and stools were flying around the room and crashing into everything. A man came running up out of nowhere and threw a brick through the front window. Most of the party goers ran out of the bar when the commotion started, but some of Patty's loyals stayed to fight. It was a bad choice. They were pummeled with fists and boots as flannelled chests trudged around the room relentlessly. It was complete mayhem.

This wasn't what Stacio wanted, but there was nothing he could do about it now. He backed against a wall and pleaded through the insanity. "Stop this… please," he begged, ducking to avoid a flying stool.

The stool hit the wall behind him and exploded into splinters. Chairs flew over the bar. Patty and his brothers ducked. Bottles and glasses broke. Mirrors shattered. Patty cringed.

Out front, Denny could barely restrain a frightened Chestnut as she kicked and neighed.

"Easy, girl, relax," he whispered, trying to see what was happening through the massive hole in the storefront window.

As the melee settled, a busted Tiffany chandelier wobbled back and forth from the highest point in the bar. The irate congregation couldn't find anything else, or anyone else to break, so they stopped.

The establishment was completely destroyed, it looked like the building was flipped upside down. As the vigilantes began to clear out, only heavy breathing and crunching debris could be heard through the tense silence.

Patty stood up slowly from behind the register. "My bar," he said, looking around at the devastation, "it's gone."

Anger, pain, and sadness overwhelmed Patty all at once. "I'll kill ya," he screamed, slamming his fists down on the bar. "You're dead, Iceman. Dead!"

Stacio stood there, unfazed. He was sorry for the mess, but not at all sorry for the man. Patty was thirsty for revenge, jumping up and trying to climb over the bar. Stacio took a step forward, raising his fists and waiting for the Champ to come to him. Kenny and Richie pulled Patty down and held him back.

"You came looking for a fight, old guy?" Patty yelled, spitting and slashing at the air. "Now, you got one."

Father Henry wiped blood from his mouth and took a step forward. "New Year's Eve, Comiskey Park, four o'clock," he said, "12 ounce gloves, Queensbury rules enforced by an impartial ref."

"You got it, Priest," said Patty, "and you better bring a coffin for your brother. He'll be needing it."

Stacio stood with his jaw open, speechless. He couldn't believe Patty had agreed to the terms of the fight. Father Henry winked at

Stacio as he walked toward the exit. "We got him," he whispered.

Denny giggled with excitement, holding Chestnut's reins with one hand and jotting notes in his pad with the other. *This Iceman's one crazy son of bitch*, he thought, sliding his pad back into his breast pocket.

The next morning, Patty sat in Marty's office, waiting like a child about to be scolded by his parents. He stood up and walked toward the closet, stopping halfway to touch a poster hanging on the wall. He ran his hands down the bare-chested image of himself and said, "We're gonna hurt this old guy... really bad."

Patty laughed as he opened the closet door and grabbed a putter. "But, he asked for it."

Marty stormed into the room and slammed down another newspaper. "Look at this shit," he screamed, jamming his finger at the headline as he read, "Iceman gets revenge. Champ's joint busted up. Fight is set."

Marty looked like he was going to have a nervous breakdown. Patty stood there, smiling and putting a golf ball into a paper cup.

"Look at me," Marty said. "Are you out of your mind?"

Patty swung the putter over his shoulder, he looked up at his manager and said, "All my life, Marty, I've dreamed of one thing. I dreamed of owning my own spiffy nightclub. My very own bar with my name on a sign in fancy lights. I had it, Marty, I finally had it. Until some Polak iceman, and his Polak priest of a brother came along and busted up the joint. They really busted it to hell. Did you see it, Marty?" he asked. "It's bad."

"What do you care," Marty asked, "you could buy a dozen more bars tomorrow if you wanted to."

"I care because that was MY place," said Patty, tapping his chest, "mine. I loved that place. That was supposed to be the place where it all began."

"Listen, Patty, I'm sorry about your bar," he said, "but you absolutely cannot fight this tomato can. There's just no way."

Patty laughed, "The fight's already set, Marty. Don't you read the papers?"

Chapter Twenty-five

Morons always love an underdog

A few days later at Saint Anthony's, Father Henry stood in the center

of the ring with his brother. Turning his back to Stacio, he took a

knee and reached into a burlap sack. He carefully removed

something from the bag and stood up. Father Henry had an

uncharacteristically wicked smirk on his lips.

Stacio took a step back, nervous. "I haven't seen you make that

face since we were boys," he said. "What are you up to?"

"I'll tell you, but you won't like it," said Father Henry, hiding

whatever it was behind his back.

Stacio stretched his neck to peek around his brother, but Father

Henry hid his hands well.

"It's the infamous pin cushion, Stash," Jimmy yelled from a

heavy bag across the room, "and it hurts like hell. You better bob fast and weave even faster."

"You're not really going to hit me with that?" Stacio asked, tipping his palms up.

Without warning, Father Henry jumped forward and swung the pincushion at his brother's head. It was about the size of a baseball, with hundreds of sewing needles protruding from its body like an evil porcupine. Stacio dodged the first swipe, but Father Henry caught him in the cheek with his backswing.

"Ah," Stacio yelped, "are you crazy?"

"You should listen to Jimmy," said Father Henry. "I will teach you how to bob and weave. I don't care if your face looks like a wine cork. You will learn."

Father Henry took a few more swings at Stacio, but he bobbed and weaved around them.

"You're doing better already," he laughed. "The pincushion proves to be very motivating."

Later that night, Jimmy and Stacio sparred in the ring. After one of the early rounds, Stacio returned to his corner with a bloody nose.

"That was just a love tap," said Father Henry, "and you're bleeding like a stuck pig."

"It's nothing. I'm fine."

"No," said Father Henry, grabbing him by the glove, "come with me."

Father Henry filled the bathroom sink with warm water. "Every night I want you to fill up your basin. Add a half cup of salt and inhale the water through your nose. It hurts at first, but it works wonders."

"What does it do?"

"After about four weeks, I could smash your nose with a hammer and it won't bleed a single drop."

In Chicago's City Hall, Marty and Father Henry sat across from each other at a long conference table. The mayor sat at the head, with a few of his aides spread throughout the room. Father Henry and Marty argued back and forth while the mayor pinched the bridge of his nose and shook his head. He was running out of patience.

"The boxing commission will never sanction a fight at some baseball field," said Marty.

"Do you want them to fight in the street?" Father Henry asked. "Because that's what it will come to."

"Your brother has zero professional fights," said Marty. "He's not ranked, and he's forty-something years old. It's gonna be a bloodbath."

"A bloodbath is something we're willing to risk," said Father Henry, "and Stacio has no interest in the title, so being ranked serves no purpose."

"It's not gonna happen," said Marty.

The mayor couldn't listen any longer. He stood from his seat and slammed his fist on the table. "This fight will happen. It must be settled," he said, waving his hand in frustration. "I have kids fighting in school because of this mess. Polish attacking the Irish. Irish attacking the Polish. It's gotten out of control."

"The Poles are threatening to strike at the mills," said one of the aides.

"I heard two women tore each other's hair out at the laundromat yesterday," the mayor said, sitting down hard in his chair. "The city hasn't seen this much violence since the North and Southside gangs clashed. This writer, Lewis, he's got everybody stirred up real good. It's madness, and it must end."

"What if this guy gets killed?" Marty asked, looking around the room.

"He can handle himself," said Father Henry.

"What if he gets brain damage or something like that?" Marty asked, leaning in toward the mayor. "The Champ is in a no-win situation, sir."

The mayor lifted a hand to his clean shaven chin. He mulled it over what for a few moments before turning to Father Henry. "Can you get him a fight? I need to see if he can defend himself. I want this fight to be over and done with as soon as possible so I can get this city back in order, but I can't let him tangle with O'Banion if he can't defend himself."

"I understand, sir," said Father Henry. "One fight?"

"One fight, " said the mayor. "One good fight"

"And no pushovers," said Marty.

"Fine," said Father Henry.

"And if your brother loses?" the mayor asked.

"He won't," said Father Henry.

"If he loses, the fight's off," said Marty.

"Agreed," said Father Henry.

"I've filed an appeal with the boxing commission, but I doubt they'll touch this, especially since the Champ wants the fight to happen," said Marty, looking around the room with sincere eyes. "But we should all be praying the Iceman loses this fight, because putting him in the ring with Patty is a death sentence. It's gonna end bad for everybody. Just take some time and think about reconsidering, Father. please."

"The fight is set, and Stacio will be ready," said Father Henry. "I have the full support of the Comiskey family, and the venue's already been booked. Regardless, the church needs no blessing from the boxing commission as it'll be a charitable exhibition sponsored by the parish."

"That all sounds great and I'm completely on board, "said the mayor. "A few hundred people giving back to the community, making the best out of a terrible tragedy. I like it. You have the city's full cooperation, Father."

Father Henry nodded at the mayor. "Thank you, sir."

Marty slammed his briefcase shut and stormed out of the room.

Two weeks later, at the Chicago Armory, Stacio was getting prepared for his first professional fight. The place was at max capacity. You could barely see the ring through the cloud of smoke, as almost every man there was puffing on a cigar. The mayor and a few of his aides were in the crowd, smoking, mingling, and waiting for the action. Bets were being taken throughout the arena and nobody seemed to like the Iceman's chances of walking out of the ring on his own two feet.

In the dressing room, Jimmy was taping up Stacio's hands. Father Henry was pacing nervously, but Stacio remained calm and focused.

"Dusty Walker is a seasoned fighter," said Father Henry. "He was once ranked in the top five."

"Top three," Jimmy interrupted.

"Better yet, top three," he said, correcting himself. "So this man has class.

"I understand," said Stacio.

"He used to be Patty O'Banion's sparring partner," said Jimmy.

"True, we may be able to learn something from him," said Father Henry. "He's now long in the tooth, but he's still five or six years younger than you are."

Stacio scrunched his eyebrows and nodded.

Father Henry started to laugh, "Crazy, huh? How do you feel about that? Old?"

"Any old horse has one good kick left in him," Stacio said, with a straight face.

Jimmy and Father Henry laughed, but Stacio didn't find his age to be humorous.

Marty and the mayor were together at ringside. Armed cops who were scattered in the crowd around them were serving as the mayor's protection detail for the night. They sat and waited, chatting with all the other important people that had ringside seats. Though he'd never label himself as important, Denny Lewis was also ringside, standing in the media section directly behind the judges.

A large black man climbed into the ring and slid off his satin robe. Dusty Walker was big, strong, and bulging with muscle. Boxing caught up to a man quickly, and at thirty-seven years old, he was considered far past his prime, but you could never tell by looking at him. He bounced around the ring, throwing heavy punches at the smoke, splitting and scattering the thick clouds in front of him.

Stacio walked out shirtless, without a robe. Against Father Henry's wishes, he wore his work boots, cut off dungarees, and suspenders. Hundreds of Father Henry's congregation stood up and applauded as the Iceman climbed into the ring. Stacio was shocked by the attention and support from the crowd.

"You can do it, Stacio," a young man screamed.

"Yeah," screamed another guy, "let's go, Stash."

A third man began to chant, "Ice-man. Ice-man. Ice-man."

Within seconds, at least half the place was chanting together, "Ice-man. Ice-man. Ice-man."

Father Henry looked around and smiled, goosebumps covering his entire body. Denny Lewis nodded his head in approval, he was so giddy he almost danced.

Marty looked like he'd just bit into a lemon. *This is not good. They love this guy. Morons always love an underdog.*

When the bell rang, Dusty flew in and hit Stacio with a barrage of punches. Stacio absorbed each blow. Dusty backed off, circling him and pecking jabs like a vulture. Stacio kept absorbing Dusty's blows. Each time he tried to counter, he only hit Dusty's arms and elbows. Stacio grabbed onto him and clenched tight.

Marty leaned over and whispered in the mayor's ear, "I told you, he's no fighter."

When the bell rang, Stacio went to his corner and refused to sit down.

"What's wrong with you?" Father Henry asked. "Why aren't you fighting?

"I have no business to settle with this man," said Stacio, "he's done nothing to me."

Father Henry reached in and grabbed Stacio by the chin. "Listen to me, Stacio, if you lose this fight… they won't let you fight O'Banion. That's the deal. You have to win this fight, that's why we're doing this. This man is standing in your way."

Stacio pulled free and glared at his brother. "All right," he said, turning back toward Dusty.

"All right? That's it?" Father Henry mumbled to himself. "Great, glad I could help."

When the bell rang, Stacio walked calmly toward Walker. Dusty lunged in and threw a left cross. Stacio ducked and countered with a vicious right hook to the body. Dusty gasped, but couldn't find air. His face drained and his knees buckled. Like lightning, Stacio reloaded and threw another right hook, this time to the head. The blast shattered Walker's nose. Blood sprayed the judges and the ringside crowd as Dusty Walker's back smacked the canvas.

"Jesus Christ," Denny howled, checking his shirt for blood.

The entire room froze as the ref started to count. Marty was stunned, sitting in his seat with a cigar dangling from his lips. The mayor looked at him, then back to the ring.

"I think he can handle himself, all right," he said, patting Marty on the back.

Marty's cigar fell in his lap, snapping him out of his daze. He snuffed it out and looked back up as the bell sounded. The ref pushed Stacio toward his corner and raised his right hand in victory. The crowd erupted in celebration. Marty looked terrified.

"Yes! Yes," said the mayor, standing to applaud, "I am certainly satisfied with that."

Stacio leaned over the top rope and looked at Jimmy. "It's over?" he asked.

"Yeah, I'd say it's over," Jimmy laughed. "Good job, old man."

Father Henry climbed into the ring and raised Stacio's hand again, the arena almost shook as the entire crowd began to chant, "Ice-man. Ice-man. Ice-man."

Stacio looked around, stunned. "Why are they cheering?" he

asked his brother.

"You gave the hungry mob some blood," he said.

Dusty Walker sat on a chair in his dressing room, he was getting his ribs bandaged up by his trainer. He winced at the pain in his side while holding a bag of ice over his nose.

"Still hurting?" his trainer asked.

"Yea, when I breathe," said Walker.

"Broken rib I bet. Maybe two," his trainer said, shuffling over to answer a knock at the door.

Father Henry walked into the room with Stacio following close behind.

"What do you want?" Dusty asked.

Stacio walked up to Dusty and removed his cap. "I'm sorry. I didn't want to hurt you," he said. "I didn't even want to fight you, but they left me no choice."

"No. It was no cheap shot," said Dusty, "it was clean. No big deal, mister, just another fight."

"You work?" Father Henry asked.

"Yeah, I'm a porter at the train station," he said.

"Well, if you lose any time, just come over to Saint Anthony's.

We have food for you and your family if needed."

"That's awfully kind of ya, Father." Dusty nodded his head.

Stacio replaced his cap and opened the door to leave. Father Henry followed, stopping on the threshold to look back and ask, "You sparred with the Champ for a while, right?"

"Sure did," said Dusty. "A long time ago, before all that Champ jazz."

"Any tips?" Father Henry asked.

"Oh yeah, I got plenty," he said, nodded his head. "O'Banion's a real handful. He keeps his hands up in perfect defense, all the time. He never slips and he's never sloppy. When it comes to defending that pretty face of his, he's the best of the best. He's almost impossible to counter. He's good, he's real good." Dusty looked down and shook his head. "Listen, he's the world champion for a reason, but even he has a weakness." Dusty's eyes came up to meet Father Henry's. "Your brother's got some stones for hands. If he can stay low and hit him here," he said, wincing as he pointed to his cracked ribs, "he might be able to break him down. Bust him up low like he did to me. A tiny man with an ax can chop down a redwood with the right technique. You gotta chop that man down, chop him down with rib shots and kidney shots." Dusty looked at Stacio and then back to Father Henry. "That, Father, is the Champ's only weakness. He don't like body blows, he never did."

Father Henry nodded with a grin on his face. "Thank you, Mr. Walker, and God bless."

Chapter Twenty-six

Don't ever play cards with hoodlums

Denny Lewis walked into Ubano's Restaurant. It was the weekend and the place was packed. He weaved in and out of occupied tables and went straight into the kitchen. Waiters and waitresses were running around each other and cooks were sweating over boiling pots. Denny reached into the salad bar and grabbed a crouton as he went by. He tossed it in his mouth and walked into the freezer. He passed by hanging meat and a handful of overstocked shelves before exiting at the opposite end.

Two gangsters lifted their guns and pointed them at Denny as he came through the door. "Whoa, It's just me," he said. "Take it easy."

Denny walked across a room where six Italian men in suits were playing cards. The man in the middle, the one shuffling the deck, that man was Giuseppe Ubano. The Godfather of Chicago was pushing sixty. He wore a dark gray fedora and had a cigar dangling from his lips. He spotted Denny when he reached out for an ashtray.

"Screwloose, you come to square up?" he asked, ashing his cigar before taking another puff.

"Not exactly," said Denny. "How are you doing here?"

"Down fifty, give or take a little," said Ubano. "Don't ever play cards with hoodlums, you gotta cheat just to stay even."

"I bet," said Denny. "Listen, Ubano, I need another marker. This is the last time, I swear."

Ubano packed the cards into his palm, he tapped the bottom of the deck on the table to straighten them out, and then he looked up at Denny. "How much this time?"

"A Benjamin," said Denny.

Ubano shook his head and started dealing the cards. "No way."

Denny pulled a chair up next to him and straddled it. He turned to Lou, an older man with a head full of silver hair, who had his chair pulled a few feet away from the table. He was leaning back and reading a newspaper with one leg crossed over the other. His eyes lifted to Denny when he heard his name being called.

"Lou, what are the odds for the O'Banion fight?" Denny asked.

"80-1, the old man gets massacred," said Lou.

"You should've been at that fight last week, my friend," Denny said, tapping the table in front of Ubano as he spoke.

"Dusty Walker's a washed-up junky," Ubano said, shrugging his shoulders. "Besides, I never bet the long shot. This Polak's gonna walk right into a meat grinder."

"Listen, Ubano, this Iceman has a fire in his belly," said Denny. "I mean, I was there, ringside. I watched Dusty's ribs crumble. I saw it, I heard it, I almost felt it. His nose popped like a balloon. Stacio only threw two punches. He did that with two punches." Denny held up two fingers to everyone at the table. "Two. I tell ya, this guy's a hard boiled son of a bitch."

Ubano took a long drag of his cigar and thought about what Denny was saying. *Maybe he'll get lucky for once. I doubt it, but it's bound to happen at some point.*

Denny took off his hat and pulled out his Silver Star. He examined it with loving eyes before handing it over to Ubano. "This is the only thing that I never considered hocking. It's all I have that's valuable, valuable to me, anyway. Please, hold on to it and spot me this one last time."

"If it wasn't for that Silver Star you'd be dead by now. You know that? You're in way too deep with me, Screw, there's no way you can pay me back."

"I got a feeling about this Iceman. I never had a feeling like this before," said Denny. "I gotta take this shot. This is my chance."

Ubano set down the cards and looked up at Denny. He twisted the butt of his cigar into the ashtray and shook his head. "If the Champ wins this fight, you do understand that you're buying the farm, right, Screw?"

Denny nodded. "I gotta take this shot. Got nobody to mourn me, anyway."

"I think betting on this Iceman is suicide, but it's your bet to make."

Denny tipped his hat and leaned in close to Ubano, swallowing hard as he spoke, "If the Iceman doesn't make it, do a veteran a favor?"

"Another favor, huh? What's that?" Ubano asked.

"Two shots in the head, like a gentleman." Denny pointed to his temple.

"You can trust me on two things, Screw," Ubano said, sincere, "it'll be quick, and you'll be buried with this medal." He fixed his gaze on the Silver Star, staring hard at every detail. "That's a promise."

"Thank you for that," said Denny, patting Ubano on the shoulder before standing up and walking out of the room.

"Don't mention it," said Ubano, placing the medal down on the table and picking up his cards.

Chapter Twenty-seven

Mascara stains and a white Christmas

It was a cold December on the farm. All the trees on the property were bare, except for the pines. Every animal in the surrounding woods was cuddled up somewhere, keeping warm and waiting out the winter. Michael sat alone, staring out through the front window.

"Come on, come on, come on," he mumbled to himself, playing impatient drums on his lap.

Linda walked into the room with his practice violin in her hands.

"Why do you always hide Miss Molly's violin?" he asked.

"I don't hide it from you, dear. I just don't want your father to see it."

"When can I play for Papa?" Michael asked.

"Not right now, sweetie," she said, scrunching her nose. "I'm sorry, but when you're older you'll understand."

Michael sprang up, straightening out his slouched back. "She's here. She's here. Miss Molly's here, Mama."

Linda looked out the window and saw the black Lincoln coming up the dusty road. "Here you are," she said, handing the violin to Michael. "Go set yourself up and I'll let Miss Molly in."

Michael placed the violin on his lap and wheeled himself out of the room. "Thank you, Mama."

Later that day, Linda collected eggs from the hen house. Wooden crates, stacked four high, covered all three solid walls. White hens piled into the crates, all keeping one eye on Linda. The hens knew her and trusted her, but they were naturally skittish creatures. Linda plucked fresh eggs from selective crates and piled them gently into her wicker basket.

Once the eggs were removed, she brushed out each crate and lined them with fresh newspapers. She stuffed a page into one of the crates and froze. She looked at the page in her hand for a moment, squinting her eyes. Linda walked to the door and pushed it open to shine some light on the page in her hand. It was a black and white photo of Patty O'Banion holding Molly in his arms at the club's grand opening. Linda dropped the newspaper and the basket of eggs. She took a few deep breaths and held her hand up to her mouth. "Oh, dear, lord," she whispered, staring down at the picture.

Linda walked back into the house and made herself a cup of tea. *I don't understand, it just doesn't add up.*

She stirred milk and sugar into her cup and struggled with her thoughts. The beautiful sound of violins whirled through the house, making it hard for her to focus. Michael laughed and Miss Molly complimented his playing. Linda sat with her cup of tea in one hand and her rosary in the other. She stared at the pocket doors, waiting, her mind racing while two violins played in unison.

A few minutes later, Molly slid the doors open. "See you soon, dear," she said to Michael, before sliding the doors closed. She turned to Linda. "He improves by leaps and bounds every week. He really is a natural. Such a delight."

Linda stood up and smiled, polite as always. "Thank you for saying so. We love our Michael, he's a good boy."

Molly smiled. "He sure is," she said, leaning over the bench to pack her violin.

When she bent down, her necklace dangled out of her collar. Linda reached out and gently touched the golden charm. It was two small boxing gloves. Both women looked equally as shocked and nervous.

"Molly O'Banion?" Linda asked.

Molly's eyes filled up. She took a deep breath and stumbled to the bench. She sat down and wiped her eyes before tears had a chance to fall. "Yes," she said, "I'm afraid so."

Linda brought her hands to her temples, keeping her gaze fixed on Molly. "Stacio… my husband… he… he will not welcome you in this house."

"Yes, I know," said Molly.

"Why are you here? Why are you doing this? What do you want with my son?"

"I can't take back what my husband has done." Molly tried to dry her eyes again, but this time she failed. "He's not a monster, he just has… sometimes he's… I just wanted to," Molly stuttered, fumbling her words as she became hysterical. She found strength for a moment and looked deep into Linda's eyes. "I hate him for this. I hate him for what he's done to your son, for what he's done to an innocent child. I'm so sorry."

Molly grabbed her bags and ran to the door. She turned the brass knob and yanked frantically at the latch. She could barely see a thing as tears poured down her face. Linda came behind her and placed a gentle hand on her shoulder. Molly dropped everything she was holding, she turned and wrapped her arms around Linda. She fell to her knees and buried her face into Linda's apron, her tears staining the fabric with black mascara.

"It's okay, dear," said Linda, caressing Molly's perfect hair. "Everything's going to be okay."

"Please forgive me," Molly cried.

Linda kneeled down next to her and dabbed her cheek with a tissue. "I forgive you," she said, with a warm smile.

Molly smiled back, gathering herself and getting to her feet, "I'm so sorry for that," she said, straightening out her blouse and clearing her throat. "That was very unprofessional of me. I'm very embarrassed."

"Don't be," said Linda. "It's quite all right."

"Oh my goodness," said Molly, stepping back to examine Linda, "I've ruined your apron. Please, let me replace it."

"Don't be silly," said Linda, handing her a tissue. "I have dozens of these old things."

"Ugh," Molly sighed, wiping her face. "I'm so sorry, I've been such a mess since this whole thing. I can't even imagine how you're coping."

"It takes a lot of prayer, dear," said Linda. "Come, I'll make us some tea."

Molly sat at the kitchen table. She cleaned under her eyes and blew her nose, still trying to pull herself together. Linda brought two cups of tea and set them down before pulling up a chair. These weren't just any teacups, these were Linda's porcelain collectables, she'd never even let anyone touch them before that day.

"Drink up, dear." Linda blew steam from her cup. "The tea will help calm your nerves."

"Thank you," said Molly, pointing to a broken teacup on one of the shelves. "What happened there?" she asked.

"I've collected teacups my whole life," said Linda, "I have lots of them, but that one was always my favorite."

"And for good reason," said Molly. "It's perfection."

"It used to be," said Linda. "As you can see, it recently had a visit with the floor. It was quite heartbreaking."

"I can only imagine."

Linda looked up at the refurbished teacup and shook her head.

Grandpa's heart was in the right place, but his tape job was horrific.

"It was my Grandmother's," said Linda. "I just haven't had the heart to throw it away." She walked to the shelf and picked it up, frowning. "It's a silly obsession, really. Dear, Lord, teacups. I have much bigger things to be worrying about now."

Linda took it to the other side of the kitchen. She moved slowly, studying every inch of its porcelain body. When she finished her inspection, she closed her eyes and cringed as she dropped it into the garbage can.

"I don't think it's a silly obsession," said Molly. "You have a lovely collection."

"Thank you for saying so," said Linda, smiling as she sat back down.

"I happen to share your fondness for Ćmielów Porcelain," said Molly. "I love that it's made in Poland. I have one very similar to your Grandmother's."

Linda's eyes lit up. "How did you know it was Ćmielów Porcelain?"

Molly set her tea down and spoke in a perfect Polish dialect, "Nie mam wątpliwości, że twoja Babcia była tak piękna jak ty."

The translation formed in Linda's mind, *I have no doubt your Grandmother was as beautiful as you are.*

Linda's eyes filled with tears as she reached across the table and squeezed Molly's hand. "Thank you, that was a very nice thing to say."

The two women began to converse in their native tongue. They shared laughter, then tears, and then more laughter. Despite their age disparity, they had a deep connection. They spoke like siblings who had been reunited after many years apart.

Molly blew her nose and dabbed her tears away. "Thank you, Linda," she said, "it's been so, so long. I've never had any family here. My sister died very young from tuberculosis. Then, just before the German occupation my parents sent me to New York. By the time I graduated from Julliard, they were all gone. My entire family... all of them... gone." Molly covered up her face as if she were ashamed.

"None of that is your fault, dear. You hold your head high. You did very well for yourself, your parents would be so proud." Linda poured another cup of tea. "How about I make us some blueberry crepes tomorrow?"

Molly looked up at her, stunned. "You want me to come back?"

Linda set down the teapot and looked at Molly. "You bring so much joy to my son, and Michael brings so much joy to you. I couldn't take that away from either of you. You are Michael's music teacher. That's all Stacio needs to know."

Molly was delighted, smiling from ear to ear. She stood up and moved toward Linda with open arms. Linda got to her feet, but before she could say anything, Molly wrapped her up and squeezed her. "Thank you, Linda. Thank you so much."

"You're very welcome," she said, glancing up at the clock. "Dear, Lord, it's noon already? Stacio could be home any minute."

"Oh, my goodness," said Molly, scrambling to gather her belongings.

"Let me go see if he's coming up the road," said Linda, rushing out of the kitchen.

Molly ran over to the trash can and grabbed the broken teacup. She wrapped it up in a handkerchief and shoved it into her purse. "See you tomorrow," she said, lugging her things toward the front door. "It's been years since I've had real crepes. I'm very excited."

"Bring your appetite," said Linda, holding the door open with a smile on her face. "We'll see you then, dear."

On Christmas morning, a large tree shone red and green in the corner of the family room. Stacio, Grandpa, and Michael sat around the tree. Stevie and Stanley were playing on the floor with their new toys, and Linda was serving eggnog in one of her festive aprons. Through the window, snow flurries danced down from the sky. They weaved their way through the chilly breeze, melting as they made contact with the ground.

"A white Christmas," said Grandpa.

Everyone turned their attention to the window for a moment before returning back to whatever they were doing. Stacio observed Michael, who smiled and enjoyed watching his brothers play on the floor. Stacio giggled to himself, but he had tears in his eyes. He was proud and saddened at the same time.

Michael was unfazed by the concept that he was a young boy that would never walk again. He smiled and laughed just as much as he ever did, he never let it get him down. *What an amazing boy,* Stacio thought, blinking his eyes to dry them out. This wasn't the first time Stacio got lost while marveling at his youngest son.

Michael looked up and caught his father staring. "What is it, Papa?"

Stacio sipped his eggnog and smiled. "Did you think Santa forgot about you?"

"Huh?" Michael scrunched his brow, confused.

Stacio slid a violin out from a large red stocking, Grandpa and Linda were both surprised.

Michael's face lit up. "Wow. For me?" he asked, wheeling his chair toward Stacio.

Michael reached out and Stacio handed him the violin. He caressed it and felt around, testing its sturdiness like a seasoned vet. He nodded his head in approval. "Perfect," he said, "but, Papa, where are the strings?"

"Don't worry," said Stacio, tapping the neck of the violin. "I have a friend who's going to help us with that. We should have them by next week"

"Perfect," said Michael, running his fingers over the bridge and up the neck, smiling at his very own violin. Linda coughed from the kitchen. Michael didn't get the hint, still mesmerized by the best gift he'd ever received. Linda coughed again, louder and more exaggerated, "What do you say, Michael?" she asked.

Michael snapped out of it and looked up, "Thank you so much, Papa. I love it… it's the greatest gift ever."

"Well, I think he likes it," Grandpa laughed.

Stacio smiled. It had been so long since he really smiled. Linda was delighted. She put a hand on his shoulder and Stacio placed his hand on top of hers. They shared the moment, watching Michael caress every curve on his new instrument. He'd never truly appreciated anything as much as he did that violin.

"You did good, dear," said Linda, kissing Stacio's cheek.

"We," he said, squeezing Linda's hand. "We did good."

Linda's smile widened.

"Is it true that the strings are made of cat bellies, Papa?" Stanley asked.

"Gross," said Stevie.

"Nope, not cats," said Grandpa. "Dog bellies work just fine."

Everyone laughed when the family dog lifted his head from the floor and grunted.

"Don't worry," said Stacio, "none of that is actually true. The strings really come from the bellies of little boys," he said, jumping

225

from his seat and chasing the kids around the table.

The boys screamed and laughed. Linda watched from the kitchen and melted as her entire family overflowed with joy.

Later that night, Stacio crept into the living room to check on Michael. He was sound asleep, holding his new stringless violin like a teddy bear. Stacio stood over him and smiled, admiring his youngest boy. He reached over to turn off the light, glancing at the wheelchair staged by the foot of Michael's bed. His smile faded fast as hate and pain flooded his heart. He'd forgotten. A perfect Christmas day had zoomed by and he'd forgotten what Patty O'Banion did to his son.

My poor boy, Stacio thought, sniffling and catching a tear with his thumb.

Chapter Twenty-eight

I wash my hands of it

Father Henry stood behind a heavy bag and held it with all of his might. Stacio pounded the bag so hard Father Henry could barely hang on. "You've gotten even stronger. The holiday off has served you well, brother."

Stacio didn't respond, he just kept on punishing the heavy bag, focused. He ended his brutal combo with a right cross that came directly from his hips. It traveled up his spine, through his shoulder, and rode the perfectly formed momentum through his fist. Boom! Father Henry grunted, stumbling backwards and falling on his ass.

Jimmy ran over and offered him a hand. "You okay, Father?"

Father Henry waved Jimmy off. "I'm fine. Thank you," he said, staring up at his brother with concerned eyes.

"It's like he's possessed," Jimmy mumbled.

"He is," said Father Henry. "And I don't know what to make of it."

###

Molly sat at a large, mahogany vanity, looking at herself in the mirror as she brushed her hair. Patty walked in wearing a silk robe, his hair still wet from a shower. He came up behind her and kissed the back of her shoulder. He breathed her in and said, "You smell so good, babe."

She barely glanced at his reflection, still cold and distant. Patty's shoulders slouched. "Molly," he said, pacing the room in frustration, "tell me what's going on with you."

"Nothing's going on. I'm just not in the mood."

"It's been over two months," he said, flailing his arms. "You're not in the mood for over two months?"

"I'm sorry."

Patty shook his head and said, "It's not my fault, you know."

"What's not your fault, Patrick?"

"It's not my fault that you're barren."

Molly closed her eyes and swallowed back the sting of his words. "If God intends for us to have a child, we will have one."

"Yeah, how?" he asked, pouting. "By immaculate conception?

You don't even look at me anymore."

Molly spun around and pushed against his big, hairy chest. "Give it up, Patty, it's not gonna happen," she said. "Besides, aren't you supposed to be training? Nellie's been calling here everyday looking for you."

"Training," he scoffed. "Training for what?" Patty rolled his eyes and swiped at the air in a 'forget you' motion, before walking out of the room laughing. "Training, she says."

###

A few days later, Marty pulled into Patty's gymnasium. He parked his car and sat for a few minutes, stress aging his face by the day. *This whole damn thing is bad juju,* he thought, taking a deep breath before pulling the key from the ignition.

He gazed at the bare trees beyond the building. "That damned bar. Running over a Priest's nephew. Taking a fight with this crazy Iceman. Jesus, Jesus, Jesus," Marty spoke to himself through clenched teeth, gripping the steering wheel until his knuckles cracked. He let go, wrestling a flask from his jacket pocket and taking a few hefty swigs. Marty let out a sigh of relief before sliding the flask back into its hiding spot.

Father Henry walked up to the gym's entrance and looked down at his pocket watch. He lifted his head and glanced around the parking lot.

"Father," Marty yelled, hopping out of his car and raising his hand, "I'm right over here."

Swing music engulfed the two men as they entered the gym. "Ugh, here we go," Marty mumbled.

Patty was in the middle of the ring wearing a Santa hat and a red sweatsuit. He was dancing with three beautiful, young ladies who were all infatuated with him. Richie and Kenny stood in the corner drinking beer and laughing.

"What in the hell is going on here, Patty?" Marty screamed, blood rushing to his face. "You have a fight in a few days. You're supposed to be training with Nellie."

Marty yanked the radio out of the wall, startling the three girls. They stopped dancing and backed into the far corner of the ring. Patty danced obnoxiously toward the ropes and leaned over them. "Relax, Boss, we're just having a little fun with these knockout jive-bombers," he said, turning back toward his brothers. "Ain't that right, boys?"

Kenny and Richie nodded. The three girls giggled quietly with their hands over their mouths. Marty just stood and glared at his champion. Patty bent down and picked up his beer, he took a swig and looked at Father Henry. "What brings you here, Father? Your brother finally come to his senses? He ready to chicken out?"

"No, I'm afraid not," he said. "I must confess, your method of training is a bit unorthodox."

Patty scrunched his eyebrows and pointed down at Father Henry. "Don't get wise with me, Priest. Not after what you and your freaks pulled in my bar."

Marty jumped in. "What the hell is the matter with you? Embarrassing me like this? He came here to talk to you, Patty, so let the Priest have his say."

"Thank you," said Father Henry, placing a hand on Marty's shoulder. "I've arranged to have an ambulance on duty, no easy task for a holiday, but it's done. I'm bringing in Mickey O'Sullivan, he's a well known referee from New York. He's a big man, plenty strong to pry."

"I know when to break off, Father," Patty scoffed. "I'm a pro, remember?"

"He's more for Stacio," said Father Henry.

Patty looked toward Marty, agitated. "You believe this guy? He's pushin' it, Marty."

Marty gave Patty a stern look and then turned to Father Henry. "Listen, Father, no disrespect here, but I've been in the business a long time. Don't think you can put any kind of mind twist on us."

"You're not taking my brother seriously enough," said Father Henry.

"Let me assure you of something, Priest," said Patty, leaning hard on the top rope. "Come New Year's Eve, I won't be doing any dancing. I'll just be doing a whole lot of hurting."

Father Henry stepped forward and grabbed the bottom rope. He looked up at Patty, overflowing with sincerity as he pleaded, "Please, Patty, do not fight Stacio. Just apologize to my nephew. Please. This can all end peacefully."

"After you destroyed my place?" Patty frowned. "No chance. I think I'll rough him up just for fun now."

"Please," Father Henry begged, placing a gentle hand on Patty's boot. "Just apologize. This has gone too far, and it will only end badly."

Patty glared down at him, his nostrils flaring. He set his jaw and kicked the Priest's hand away. He looked at his brothers and poked a thumb toward Father Henry. "Drag this clown out of here, will ya."

Kenny and Richie stood up straight and looked at each other. "He's a priest, Patty, we can't be dragging him anywhere," said Kenny.

"Yeah, Patty, I'm not touching no priest," Richie said. "That's more Hail Mary's than I can handle in a lifetime."

Patty's blood boiled. He leaned over the ropes to get closer to Father Henry. "I'm gonna put your thick-headed, Polak brother in that ambulance. Real fast, and real hard. That's no threat, that's a promise, Priest." Patty turned back to his brothers. "Walk him outta here gently if you want to, I don't give a damn," he said, waving his hands in frustration, "just get him out of my sight. Now."

Kenny walked over and respectfully turned Father Henry toward the door. "I'm sorry, Father, but you gotta go."

Kenny was firm and steady, but not rough. Father Henry struggled to turn around, breathing hard as he wrestled free to look back at Patty. "I am an agent of peace," he yelled, "I may have failed here today, but I did not fail in training my brother." Kenny loosened his grip and let Father Henry speak. "Stacio is old, true, but he's fit for the task at hand. The spirit of vengeance has possessed him, pushed him, and changed him. I don't even recognize him anymore. I must assure you, Patty, come New Year's Eve, I'll be unleashing a dog from hell."

Marty looked stunned by the priest's words. Richie and Kenny were disturbed, and the three young ladies turned pale with fear. Priests didn't say things like that under any circumstances. Father Henry wasn't playing intimidation games, he was truly intimidated himself.

Marty closed his eyes and pinched the bridge of his nose. *This shit storm just gets worse and worse.*

Patty was the only one in the room smiling. It wasn't a happy smile, though, it was more of an, 'I'm about to do something bad' smile. Patty took a huge swig of his beer, and before Marty could say anything, Patty leaned over the ropes and spit right in Father Henry's face. Beer and foam soaked the front of him, and everyone's jaws hit the floor.

"For crying out loud," Marty screamed.

"Get him out of here. Now," Patty screamed back.

Marty handed Father Henry a handkerchief. "I'm deeply sorry, Father, I have no words."

Father Henry wiped the beer from his face and spoke loud enough for the room to hear, "I am innocent of this man's blood. Like Pilate… I wash my hands of it, and my conscience is clear. God bless all of you."

"Get lost, already," Patty laughed, jogging around the ring and throwing quick combinations at the air. "Let's go, Richie."

Richie walked into the center of the ring with boxing pads held up. Patty hit the pads with lightning fast punches, laughing and taunting the priest. Father Henry just shook his head as he walked out of the gymnasium.

"Set the bucket there," said Stacio, brushing Chestnut's mane with one hand and pointing to the floor with the other.

Stanley set the bucket of oats down and Chestnut began to eat.

"That's a good girl," said Stacio.

"She loves it." Stanley smiled.

"Yes, she does," said Stacio, grabbing a pitchfork and scraping a layer of hay from a bale. "Never buy from Santini. Always go to

Straus' farm, he has a nice mix of alfalfa." Stacio looked at Stanley, who was daydreaming. "You hear me? And never pay more than fifteen cents a bale."

"Why are you telling me this?" Stanley asked.

"You'll be fifteen soon," said Stacio, "and these are things you need to learn."

"Are you telling me this because your fight's coming up?"

Stacio ignored his son's question.

"Can I come to the fight?" he asked. "I wanna cheer you on."

"No," said Stacio. "It's no place for a boy. Just remember what I told you."

"Go to Straus. Fifteen cents a bale. I got it."

"Good," said Stacio, patting his son on the back.

Chapter Twenty-nine

New Year's Eve

New Year's Eve was the peak of a brutally cold winter in Illinois. Thousands of people were huddled together, struggling to stay warm while trying to get into Comiskey Park. The line weaved in and out of city blocks, stretching over a mile into snowy Chicago.

The police were overwhelmed by the size of the crowd. Nobody, not even Marty, had ever seen a crowd so large. The cops tried to keep it organized, only letting a few people in at a time as the line crept slowly toward the entrance. Everyone was bundled up in hats, scarves, gloves, and thick, winter coats. Smoke seemed to be dancing from people's mouths, an endless stream of breath rising and fading into the crisp air.

Ushers from Saint Anthony's Cathedral stood at the gates, extending offering baskets to the crowd as they poured in. They were filling up quickly as almost everyone tossed something in as they walked by. You could feel the energy inside the park, people were revved up. Even though they were near frozen solid, they blew into their hands, shook out their feet, and stood their ground. A Chicago winter was tough, but on this night, the people in Chicago were even tougher. It didn't matter if you were from Chicago, it didn't matter if you were Polish, Irish, or otherwise. No one wanted to miss this fight.

When booking Comiskey Park, nobody, not Father Henry, Marty, the mayor, Stacio; not even Patty O'Banion himself considered any kind of following. Just 'a couple hundred people giving back to the community,' like the mayor said, right? Wrong. When news about this fight broke, it snowballed its way across America like you wouldn't believe. Celebrities, writers, actors, the biggest jazz musicians, pro fighters, ball players, and even politicians came from all around the country to see the Iceman avenge his boy. Tens of thousands of people showed up, it was incredible. It didn't matter who you were, anybody who was anybody was spending New Year's Eve at Comiskey Park.

Drunken revelers sipped from brown paper bags, blowing their horns and screaming for blood. The poor and working class stood in the outfield, grandstands, and up in the bleachers. Men loaded logs, sticks, and brush into metal barrels out in center field. The crowd flocked as the fires lit up. People reached their hands toward the flames, desperate for the slightest flicker of warmth.

The boxing ring sat in the center of the baseball diamond. Ten men worked inside the ring, sweeping away snow, toweling the mat, and chipping icicles off of the ropes. Hundreds of cars, mostly Cadillacs and Lincolns, were parked around the ring. The idling engines exhausted smoke that billowed like rooftop chimneys. Anyone with any kind of money would be able to watch the fight up close and personal from the comfort of their very own heated automobile.

Father Henry paced back and forth in the dressing room, biting at his thumb nail and taking overly deep breaths. Stacio was lying down on a bench by the lockers with his eyes closed. He was already taped up and dressed, he seemed relaxed and focused.

Jimmy walked in, excited. "There's gotta be twenty-thousand people out there, Father, and there's still a mob of people trying to get in," he said, pointing a thumb toward the door. "The mayor said to take our time."

"Twenty-thousand?" Father Henry asked, shocked.

"Maybe more," said Jimmy.

"All right, then," said Father Henry, "let's get the grease on him."

Stacio opened his eyes and sat up. "It's after three o'clock. I'm ready."

Father Henry turned toward his brother and said, "You need the Vaseline, Stacio. It will keep…"

"I don't need it," Stacio interrupted.

"Stash, it'll keep the heat from escaping your skin," said Jimmy. "It's real cold out there. You're gonna want it."

"I don't need it," Stacio repeated. "Let's go."

Jimmy looked at Father Henry and shrugged his shoulders. Father Henry shrugged back and took another deep breath. "It's settled, then," he mumbled. "Let's go."

Stacio marched through a long, dark tunnel. Jimmy and Father Henry were nearly jogging to keep up. Light crept closer to the Iceman with every step he took toward the mouth of the tunnel. Darkness fell farther behind the three men with every clunk of Stacio's work boots. His shins became illuminated, revealing the bottoms of his cut-off dungarees. The rest of him was a ghostly

silhouette, moving with a fierce sense of urgency. Clunk. Clunk.

Clunk. Stacio was halfway to the light at the end of the tunnel. Father

Henry and Jimmy trailed behind him. Clunk. Clunk. The light

reached just under Stacio's shoulders, revealing bare skin with

suspender straps looping over his shoulders and running down his

back.

Jimmy and Father Henry ran to each side of him. Wind howled

through the opening of the tunnel. When they were still ten feet from

the exit, the wind gusted so violently that a fine mist of snow shifted

direction and blasted all three of them. Father Henry reached for

Stacio's shoulder, but he missed, and Stacio kept on marching.

Clunk. Clunk. Clunk. Jimmy was bundled up in a heavy pea coat

with a ski mask and gloves. Father Henry was wearing a dense, wool

jacket with a scarf, earmuffs, and gray mittens. All three of the men's

breath rose like thick smoke over a bonfire.

They were mere inches from the exit now, and when the light

revealed Stacio's eyes, Jimmy and Father Henry caught another

glimpse of a man possessed. His gaze was fixated. He stared through

the mouth of the tunnel like his destiny was waiting for him on the other side. Wasn't it, though? Stacio was a simple man. He had never wanted anything as much as he wanted this fight. It was so close he could almost taste it. Win, lose, or draw, he would make Patty O'Banion pay for what he'd done to Michael, and if he couldn't, he was fully prepared to die trying.

Father Henry reached out again and grabbed Stacio by the shoulder. Stacio stopped and turned to his brother.

"Here, put this on," said Father Henry, holding a robe open in front of him. "You're gonna catch pneumonia before the bell rings."

"No, I don't need it," he said. "I just want to get out there and settle this."

"No grease. No robe. No boxing gear whatsoever," Jimmy laughed. "This guy's tough as nails. He's gonna win this fight for crying out loud, isn't he?"

Father Henry rolled his eyes in frustration. "Let's just hope he doesn't get hypothermia before it starts," he said, tossing the robe down and waving his hand toward the exit. "After you, little brother."

When Stacio emerged from the tunnel, the crowd erupted. It caught all three men by surprise. Stacio turned to Father Henry and asked, "What is this?"

"They believe in what you're fighting for, Stacio. As do we," Father Henry said, pointing to himself and then Jimmy. "You fight to protect the weak. Because of that, I have no doubt that God will be in your corner."

Father Henry crossed Stacio with the Holy Trinity before pulling him in for a hug. He kissed him on the forehead and looked deep into his burning eyes. Stacio stared back at his brother for a few moments, and then both men nodded their heads in a silent understanding.

"For Michael," said Father Henry.

"For Michael," Stacio replied.

"For Michael," Jimmy yelled, smacking both men on their backs before leading the way toward the ring.

Jimmy forced himself through the rowdy mob, spreading people apart with both arms extended. Stacio lowered his head and tucked in behind him, while Father Henry tried his best to keep the crowd off his brother. Everyone wanted to put a hand on Stacio, he was like a celebrity to the Polish community, and a hero to the working class. The people loved him. When they finally reached the ring and Stacio climbed inside, the park went wild again. Cars honked their horns and flashed their lights, the crowd cheered so loud that the ring rumbled under Stacio's boots. He walked to all four corners and observed the audience, blown away by the support.

Stacio went back to his corner and leaned on the ropes. "Where did all of these people come from?" he asked his brother.

"Everywhere," said Father Henry.

"Dear, Lord, please stay close to my husband," Linda whispered, kneeling down in her pew at an empty Saint Anthony's Cathedral.

A thin slice of light pierced through the church's dim foyer as someone slipped inside. Linda didn't notice, continuing to pray with her head down. The soft clacking of high heels approaching finally grabbed her attention. She lifted her head to find Molly standing over her.

"May I?" Molly asked, pointing to the empty spot next to Linda. Linda nodded her head and smiled.

"It's been quite some time since I've been to church," Molly confessed. "My wedding day was the last time, I'm ashamed to say."

"Really?" Linda asked. "I don't think I've ever missed a Sunday mass. Not since my teens, anyway."

Molly looked at her, impressed, her eyes studying Linda a moment too long before she mumbled, "How? How do you do it?"

Linda took a deep breath and smiled. "Faith is so important. I just love the feeling of…"

"No, not that," Molly interrupted. "How do you forgive? How do you refrain from hating me?"

"Molly, dear, hate has no place in my heart," said Linda. "First of all, this was not your fault. Secondly, I would never blame you or any other wife for something her husband has done. Being Christian is helping people, saving people if you can. You're a wonderful soul, and you needed saving just as much as my Michael did." Linda placed her hand on top of Molly's and continued, "The two of you needed each other, and there is nothing left to forgive here. I cannot speak for my husband, but I am thankful for you, and for the joy that you've brought to my child. Regardless of who's right or wrong, our husbands each believe in what they're fighting for. Even so, that has nothing to do with us."

Molly used her thumbs to catch tears before they could ruin her makeup again. "But a simple apology," she said. "How could it possibly be enough?"

"I don't know that it would've been enough, dear, but it would've been something," Linda said. "It's not my job to know why an apology was so important to my husband, just like it's not your job to know why an apology was too much to ask of yours. They're men, and they have a different way of thinking. All I can do is come here and say a prayer for the man I love, so that's what I do."

"Do you mind if I pray with you?" Molly asked.

"Not one bit," said Linda, grabbing Molly by the hand and guiding her into the pew.

The two women shared a brief hug before Linda leaned away to examine her. She wiped a tear from Molly's cheek and smiled.

Molly smiled back and said, "Thank you, Linda."

"There's no need to thank me, dear, that's what friends are for."

Molly lit up at the word 'friends'. She grabbed her purse and reached inside. "So, before I forget," she said, handing Linda her Grandmother's fully repaired, Ćmielów Porcelain teacup. Somehow, It was in mint condition. "This is a gift, from me to you."

Linda was stunned. "This can't be the same teacup."

"It certainly is," said Molly. "I had it repaired by a master potter."

Linda's eyes filled with tears. "I never thought I'd see it again," she said, running her fingers along every detail. "Thank you so much, Molly, it's perfect. I don't know how I can ever repay you for such a kind and generous gift."

"You're very welcome," said Molly. "But don't be silly, this is a gift from one friend to another. No need to reciprocate, you've done enough for me."

"Well, I appreciate that," said Linda. "This is certainly the nicest thing anyone has ever done for me, and it will never be forgotten. I don't think I could ever thank you enough," she said, pulling a handkerchief from her purse and dabbing her tears. She faced forward in her pew and smiled at Molly before bowing her head to pray. Molly admired Linda for a moment before following suit. She placed a hand over Linda's and they prayed together in silence.

"This is it? This is the big time?" Richie asked, taking a swig from a large bottle of cognac. "I expected the White Sox clubhouse to be a little bit more impressive." He tucked the bottle away and ran his hand along a row of wooden lockers.

"Just goes to show ya," said Kenny, "Patty's Place is the nicest thing this town's got goin."

"Damn right," said Patty, lying face down on a table while Nellie massaged his hamstrings.

"Take a look at this," said Richie, reaching into one of the lockers and pulling out a baseball bat. "You might need this for that thick-headed Polak out there."

Kenny, Patty, and Nellie all laughed as Richie acted like he hit himself in the head with the bat. "Bang. I'm so sorry, Champ. Bang. I'm just a crazy Iceman…"

"For goodness sake," Marty yelled, storming into the room and interrupting Richie's show. "Give me that," he said, yanking the bat from Richie and placing it back in the locker. "They didn't even want to let us use this locker room. We are not to touch anything. Got it?"

"Yeah, jeez, Marty, what the hell's your problem?" Richie asked, holding his arms out to his sides.

"What's my problem?" he asked. "This entire thing's been nothing but a circus." Marty paced the room nervously. "And there you are, front and center as always, making ME look like a Goddamn clown."

"Whoa, whoa, whoa," said Richie. "You better just take a deep breath and tone it down before you get yourself a smack."

Marty flailed his arms in the air and said, "This is what I gotta put up with."

Patty lifted his head from the table and said, "Aye, Richie. How many times do I gotta tell ya not to talk to Marty like that? Come on, Marty, he didn't mean that."

"All right, all right, everybody relax," said Kenny. "We all know the runt has behavioral issues. Don't take it personally."

"I'll show you a runt, Kenneth," Richie snapped back. "And you," he said, pointing to Patty. "I didn't even say nuttin bad to the geezer."

"Richie," Patty yelled, "you just called him a geezer."

"Yeah, but that was after," he yelled back. "And he is a geezer."

"Just don't aggravate him," said Patty. "You know he's high strung. I don't need you giving my manager a heart attack."

"I'm not high strung," said Marty. "The three of you could drive anyone nuts."

"He meant to say 'the two of you'," said Kenny.

"Yeah, that's exactly what I meant," said Marty, sarcastically.

"Told ya," said Kenny, standing up and leaving the room.

Marty looked down at his golden pocket watch and said, "It's four o'clock, let's get going before the sun sets. I'm gonna go take a quick peek, I'll be right back. Don't touch anything, Richie. I mean it," he said, eyeing Richie down as he left the room.

Richie bit his tongue and sat down, rolling his eyes as he took another gulp of cognac.

"He's a stress case, Richie, just stay out of his way," said Patty. "Thanks for not getting into it with him just now."

"Wasn't easy," said Richie.

"I know he's a pain in the ass sometimes," said Patty, "but he's done alot for this family. You know?"

"Yeah, you're right," said Richie. "He is a pain in the ass."

Patty, Richie, and Nellie all shared a laugh.

When Kenny returned, a wave of frozen air rushed in behind him. He wasn't out there very long, but his eyes already looked wind burned and bloodshot. He tried to shake off the cold, blowing into his hands and tapping his feet on the floor. "It's bad news bears out there," he said.

"What's going on?" Patty asked.

"The Iceman's out there waiting for ya," said Kenny. "The crowd's getting restless, and the snow's getting heavier."

Marty came in through another door, followed by a second rush of arctic air.

"A lot of people show up?" Patty asked.

"A lot of people?" Marty scoffed.

"Patty, I ain't never seen so many people before," said Kenny.

"More people than the Chamber's rematch in New York?" Nellie asked.

"Double that, at least," said Marty.

Patty sat up on the table and hung his legs over the edge. "Are you guys joking with me?" Patty looked shocked. "Double the Chamber's rematch? There's no way. There was like twenty-thousand people in Madison Square Garden."

Marty made the sign of the cross over himself. "Patty, I swear on my mother's grave, I've never seen a crowd anywhere near this before."

"Ready for this one?" Kenny asked, pointing a thumb back over his shoulder. "The cop was just telling me that the line is still four blocks long."

"Unbelievable," Marty mumbled under his breath.

"Four blocks, huh?" said Patty. "Then let the sucker wait. I want the whole city to see me crush this old man. I wanna show everybody what happens when you mess with the O'Banions."

"Alright, then start jumping rope," said Marty. "I want you loose. It's freezing cold out there, and trust me, you are not gonna like it."

Kenny tossed Patty the jump rope. Patty set it aside and reached out to Richie. "Give me a swig of the cognac."

Marty shook his head and walked away. Richie looked at Kenny for approval, but Kenny just stood there with his arms crossed like a disappointed father.

"Hey, Champ, if this fight goes anywhere, you could get dehydrated," Nellie said.

"The cognac," Patty demanded. "I wasn't asking."

Richie untwisted the cap and handed the bottle to Patty. Patty took two hefty swigs and winced. "That should warm me right up. Now, where's my red hat?"

Stacio stood patiently in the center of the ring. The crowd was a dull hum, with fans occasionally cheering, yelling, or blowing horns.

The crowd gave a light round of applause when the referee emerged from one of the tunnels. Mickey O'Sullivan was a large, bald man in his fifties. He was bundled up in a navy blue coat and black earmuffs.

He approached Stacio. "I don't know where he is," said O'Sullivan. "He should've been out here by now. Do you want a coat or a robe?"

"No, thank you," said Stacio. "I'll just wait."

The sun began to set, crouching down behind the stadium walls and forfeiting the battle against this unrelenting tundra. One of the idling cars flipped on its headlights, and then every car in the stadium did the same. The boxing ring was illuminated like a stage on Broadway. Stacio and O'Sullivan shaded their eyes and looked out into the massive crowd. Constant shadows from the falling snow provided some relief against the barrage of lights shooting in from every direction.

Sudden gusts of wind blew the snow sideways, causing it to sting when hitting bare skin. O'Sullivan shielded his face with an arm, but like an ivory statue, the Iceman stood perfectly still.

"Brother, you should warm up," said Father Henry.

Stacio replied without breaking his gaze away from O'Banion's tunnel, "I'm warm enough."

The shivering crowd was getting more aggravated with every minute that passed. "Where's our fight?" a spectator yelled.

"You too dumb to tell time or what," yelled another. "Get your ass out here, O'Banion."

Small gangs of men began tearing the bleachers apart for firewood, as more people pushed their way toward the flaming barrels. Idling cars began honking their horns with impatient excitement. The crowd was getting bigger, stronger, and more agitated every second the Champ made them wait. This was a recipe for disaster, and everyone felt it. The cops were so cold and outnumbered, they retreated back to their squad cars.

Patty was up and jumping rope in his red and white Santa hat. He huffed and puffed, building up a nice sweat.

"That's enough," said Marty. "It's getting late, we gotta go."

"Give me another sip," said Patty, waving Richie over.

Richie walked up and attempted to squirt water into Patty's mouth. Patty pushed his hand away and reached into his coat. He grabbed the bottle of cognac and took another gulp. He winced and blew out a long breath, "It's showtime."

The mayor rolled down the window of his Cadillac and waved over one of his patrolmen. "Get the state police out here," he said. "I'll pay the overtime. If we have a riot with a crowd this size, they'll take down the whole damn city."

"Sorry, sir, no can do on the help," the patrolman said, shielding his face from the whipping snow. "They told us to go to hell. It's a holiday, we're on our own out here."

"Very well, then. Go keep warm," said the mayor, nodding his head toward the patrol car. "But, stay alert."

"You got it, sir."

Ubano and his crew had a front row seat from the comfort of a well-heated Lincoln Town Car. The windshield wipers swished back and forth, clearing the snow as fast as it landed.

"Where the hell is this guy?" Ubano mumbled, cracking his window as he lit a cigar.

Ubano, two of his higher-ups, Lou and Franky, and their driver, Vito, were all waiting impatiently, cringing at the sight of a frozen Stacio in the center of the ring.

"Get a gander at that," said Franky. "This guy must be touched in the head or something."

"He hasn't moved an inch in about an hour," said Ubano, impressed. "Screwloose was right about this guy, he's a tough son of a bitch."

"Of course he's tough," said Lou, lighting his own cigar. "What'd ya expect, Boss, he's an iceman."

Ubano raised his eyebrows and nodded in agreement. "Lou, wasn't your Nonnucio an iceman?" he asked.

"He sure was," said Lou. "That man's grip was like a silverback gorilla. Still, to this day, that's the toughest bastard I ever met."

Back at the farmhouse, Michael was sitting by the front window watching snow accumulate on the sill. He sniffled as a single tear ran down his cheek.

Grandpa came into the room with a newspaper in his hand. "I saved the funnies for you, Michael." He stopped in his tracks when he saw that Michael was crying. "What's wrong, boy?"

Michael wiped his tears away with his sleeves. "Nothing's wrong, Grandpa."

"Don't lie to me," said Grandpa, puffing his pipe and leaning in toward his grandson. "What is it?"

"Well… I used to really love sledding," Michael said, drying his eyes and composing himself. "I know I'll never go sledding again, not like I used to, anyway. It's just a little sad, is all."

It took every ounce of strength Grandpa could muster to fight off the tears that were welling up in his eyes. He set down his pipe, never breaking his gaze away from Michael. "I can open the window," he said, his voice trembling.

Grandpa pulled up the window sash and a gust of wind almost blew Michael's chair back. Snow shot into the house and the curtains did a violent dance.

"We can make snowballs," said Grandpa, desperately gathering snow from the sill and packing it into his palm. He held the snowball out to Michael. "Go on, give it a throw," he said, pleading with his heartbroken eyes.

Michael looked down at the snowball, then back up at Grandpa.

Please, take the snowball, Michael. Grandpa begged, but only in his own head. *Please, don't ever cry again, I don't think I can handle it. I'm a tough old man, but no one is tough enough for this. I know you'll never sled again, you'll never walk again, either. I know it's my fault, I hate myself for this. Please, Michael, just take the snowball. This is all that I can offer you, Grandson. Please, take it and forgive your Grandfather. He loves you very much, Michael. I... I love you very much. I'm so sorry, sweet boy, I would give anything to switch places with you.*

Although Grandpa didn't say a single word out loud, Michael could almost hear him. Better yet, Michael could feel his Grandfather's words through the guilt and desperation radiating off of him.

He reached out and took the snowball. He tossed it out the window and looked back at Grandpa. "Take me to Papa," he said. "Take me to the fight."

Grandpa closed the window, scratching his head while he pondered Michael's request. "Well... I guess I'll go get your coat, but this has to be our little secret."

"Okay, Grandpa." Michael smiled, pulling an imaginary zipper across his lips.

Grandpa smiled back as he shuffled toward the closet. *Linda's gonna have my head for this one.*

Chapter Thirty

A cold day in hell

The crowd erupted when Patty and his crew emerged from the tunnel. Patty wore a white, mink robe with his Santa hat pulled down to his eyebrows. The rest of his entourage was bundled up in coats, gloves, and hats. He didn't show it, but Patty felt the painful chill in the air. The crowd was a loud mix of cheers, boos, and horns, honking and blowing relentlessly. As the ice-cold walk to the ring seemed to last forever, the crowd began to chant, "Fight! Figh! Fight!"

Patty and Nellie climbed into the ring together. "Don't toy with him, Patty, let's make it quick and get the hell outta here," Nellie begged, rubbing his frozen hands together.

Patty disrobed, jumping up and down to stay warm and loose. He turned and stomped to the center of the ring. He bore down on Stacio, who was still standing in the same spot. Patty was the much larger man, towering him in height and dwarfing him in width.

Stacio stood his ground, though, unfazed by him or the blizzard. His

eyes were set on Patty, staring a hole directly through the Champ.

"You cold, Iceman?" Patty taunted. "That's all right. Once you're

asleep, you won't feel nuttin."

Stacio raised his chin, but remained silent. He was a heat-seeking

missile, and he was locked in on his target. None of Patty's antics

could break his focus now. He was ready. The Champ had a large

debt to pay off, and the Iceman was there to collect.

O'Sullivan put a hand on each man's chest and pressed himself

between them. "I want a clean fight, gentlemen. Back of the head or

below the belt, you lose a point. No elbows, no headbutts, no tripping

or kicking. I don't miss a thing. Understood?"

"Yeah, yeah, whatever you say, Chrome-dome." Patty waved the

man off with a glove and walked away.

Stacio nodded his head to O'Sullivan, he brushed the snow out of

his hair and as he walked back to his corner.

"You look like a frosty, old snowman out there," said Jimmy.

"He feels like one, too," said Father Henry, inserting Stacio's

mouthpiece. "Stay low, brother. Take short, compact swings to the breadbasket. You must control your anger to win this fight. Swing wild, and you're a goner."

One of the ringside judges went to the trunk of his car and took out a crowbar. He used it to crack ice off of the bell before it could be rung. When it did ring, the crowd cheered as the fighters moved gingerly toward each other over the sopping wet canvas. The fight was finally underway, and everyone in Comiskey Park was ready for a show.

Patty came out aggressive, throwing three quick combinations. Stacio bobbed and weaved, barely letting the punches graze him. Patty unloaded a right cross on Stacio's forehead, knocking him back onto the ropes. The entire crowd gasped in unison. Before Stacio could recoil off the ropes, Patty was on top of him throwing wild punches. Almost every shot landed on Stacio's body, but he absorbed them well, focused on protecting his head and face.

Denny Lewis pulled his scarf over his eyes. "Jeez Louise, Iceman," he said, peeking out with one eye.

Patty leaned back and exploded forward, splitting Stacio's gloves and landing a solid punch right on his chin. Stacio winced and grunted as his head whipped back on his neck. Patty slid backwards and waited for Stacio to fall, but when he didn't, Patty realized just how tough this Iceman really was.

A right cross on the chin, Patty thought, *MY right cross on the chin. A solid shot like that… right on the button… and nothing?*

That same punch had put down professional fighters. The best of the best, as a matter of fact. That same punch won O'Banion the heavyweight title when it put an undefeated Rodney Chambers to sleep in Boston a few years ago. Then, it put him to sleep a second time at Madison Square Garden for the big rematch.

Maybe it wasn't as solid as I thought. Maybe it wasn't right on the button. It could've been a little off, right? It had to be if this bozo's still standing in front of me.

"Maybe it's because you've been drinking booze instead of water," Marty's voice spoke inside Patty's head. "Or maybe it's because you messed up this time, Champ. You messed up real good this time."

"Maybe it's because you crippled a little boy and then denied his broken father a simple apology," Kenny's voice spoke, stern. "An apology that you know the boy and his family deserved."

Then Molly's voice, "What would you do, Patrick? What would

you do if someone crippled our child?"

Father Henry's voice spoke to him last, "Look what you've done. I don't even recognize my own brother. He isn't even a man anymore. He's something else now, something… unbreakable. You've created this monster, Patty, now you must answer to it. Whatever that is standing across from you, it wants you, and by God, it's going to have you."

Patty snapped out of his trance. "It ain't getting me!" he screamed, startling O'Sullivan.

The ref looked back and forth at the two men, confused as to who Patty was talking to. "You okay, Champ?"

"I ain't never been scared of nuttin," he said, turning to lock eyes with Father Henry. "Stay out of my head, Priest. I'm warning you."

Father Henry looked at Jimmy and shrugged his shoulders. O'Sullivan just nodded and brushed it off. Stacio gathered himself and raised his fists, staring at Patty with possessed eyes. Patty stared back, hate sizzling through his blood. His warm breath exhausted from his nostrils like a Brahma bull. Patty let out a growl as he charged, swinging a wild right hook that could've knocked out a grizzly bear, had it landed. Stacio ducked under the punch and threw a thunderous left hook at Patty's ribs.

Boom! The wind leaving the Champ's lungs screeched like racecar tires over blacktop. As Patty hunched over in pain, Stacio exploded from his hips with a right uppercut. The punch lifted Patty off his feet and sent him sliding on his back across the frozen canvas. The entire stadium erupted. Horns honking, lights flashing, everyone went wild. Jimmy screamed and cheered at the top of his lungs, shaking the bottom rope until he was out of breath.

Father Henry clenched his fists. "Stay down, Patty, stay down," he prayed under his breath.

Denny's jaw almost dropped to the floor, he ripped off his scarf and went wild, jumping and cheering with the man next to him. He couldn't believe Patty went down, nobody in the stadium expected that. Nobody without the last name Jasinski, anyway.

"We got us a fight, fellas," Ubano said to his crew, while Franky yelled Italian curse words out the passenger side window.

"I slipped," said Patty, jumping right back to his feet and dusting the snow off his rear end.

The bell rang and both men walked back to their corners. Patty walked backwards, never taking his eyes off Stacio. Stacio made it to his corner, his eyes searching for Father Henry. When they finally saw one another, Father Henry gave him a nod of approval.

Patty plopped down heavily onto the stool in his corner. Nellie hopped in the ring and covered him with the mink robe. "What the hell are you doing out there, Champ?"

"Nellie, I'm in there with a lunatic," said Patty, grabbing the cognac from Richie and gulping it down like water. "This guy don't feel the cold. He don't feel no pain. He don't feel nuttin."

Stacio, refusing to sit, stood in his corner and listened to his brother's advice.

"Good uppercut, Stacio, but don't even think about throwing it again. Forget the head," said Father Henry, tapping on his own ribs with both hands. "The body, Stacio, the body."

Stacio swallowed his mouthpiece and nodded.

At the bell, the fighters clashed again in the center of the ring. Patty was throwing sloppy punches, his aim wild and his balance awkward. Stacio bobbed and weaved like a pro, landing precise, compact punches on Patty's ribs, elbows, and forearms. Stacio pounded Patty back into his own corner.

"That's it, Iceman. Pow. Pow. Whack." Denny was mimicking

each blow, shadow boxing with the guy next to him.

To everyone's surprise, Patty was cowering in his corner, taking an absolute punishment to the body. Snot ran down his lips as tears built up in his eyes. His ears were blood red, and throbbing from the blistering wind. Patty couldn't take anymore. He popped up and threw a desperate elbow across Stacio's chin. Stacio stumbled back and fell to one knee.

The entire crowd began to boo Patty, even some of his own followers started jumping ship. The people in their cars laid on their horns and booed, while the people outside started whipping snowballs into the ring; all of which were aimed right for the Champ. O'Sullivan stepped between the two men, he scolded Patty and then held a finger out to the judges; who were huddled tight and bundled up under blankets and umbrellas. One of the judges nodded to the ref and made a note of the penalty.

"Keep it clean, Champ," said O'Sullivan. "I know the belt's not on the line, but you don't wanna lose that perfect record to a disqualification. Do you?"

"No sir, it was a complete accident," Patty said, raising his hands in innocence. "I swear it."

O'Sullivan gave Stacio some time to recover. When he raised his gloves and said he was ready to go, the crowd cheered.

"Fight," O'Sullivan said, sliding out of the way.

Stacio charged Patty this time, backing him into his own corner again. Patty wasn't even fighting back, he was in full defense, protecting his face and head like he was being mauled by a bear. Stacio had no interest in Patty's head anyway, unloading bomb after bomb on the Champ's body.

Patty's face was pale, his lips were blue, and all of his strength was gone. Each punch chipping away at his core like a razor-sharp shovel through soft earth. Nellie considered the towel for a moment, but he knew the Champ would rather die than quit. Just as the thought crossed his mind, Patty was saved by the bell.

"Oh, thank God," Nellie mumbled.

Patty staggered to his corner with the Iceman on his heels. "Do you have anything to tell me?" Stacio grumbled through his mouthpiece.

Patty pushed his glove into Stacio's face. "Never. I ain't sorry for nuttin," he said, and the spectators began to boo him again.

The ref grabbed Stacio and escorted him to his own corner. Patty waved Kenny over and snatched his championship belt. He raised it

over his head and taunted the crowd, "Boo all you want, peasants.

I'm the heavyweight champion of the world, and don't you forget

it!"

It took everything he had not to cry from the discomfort he felt

when lifting his arms above his head. *Son of a bitch.* Patty coughed

so hard he nearly vomited from the pain shooting down his sides. He

tossed his belt back down to Kenny and sat gently on his stool. *Shit.*

Marty jogged over and jumped into the mayor's warm Cadillac.

He tried his best to hide his concern, but it wasn't very convincing.

"Jesus, Marty, close that door," said the mayor.

"This fight's gonna be over in no time, I can promise you that,"

said Marty.

"Oh yeah, and which way do you see it going? This Iceman

didn't come here to roll over, Marty. This guy's tough."

Marty knew the mayor was right, and as much as he tried to deny

it, his eyes gave him away.

All of the priests and nuns from Saint Anthony's Cathedral were

gathered in the White Sox dugout. Everyone was thrilled to see

Michael when Grandpa wheeled him inside. They all greeted him with smiles, hugs, and words of encouragement.

"We all pray for Stacio," said one of the priests, reaching out and shaking Grandpa's hand.

"Thank you… sir," Grandpa responded awkwardly, not knowing if that was the proper verbiage to use when talking to a priest who wasn't his son. As much as Linda and Father Henry tried, Grandpa was never big on church.

Stacio walked to his corner and leaned on the ropes.

"Keep pounding the body," said Father Henry. "Just keep on pounding, Stacio."

Stacio nodded at his brother, but his focus was elsewhere. He stared out through the snow flurries and thought he saw Michael in the dugout. He squinted his eyes to see better as a nun placed a blanket over his son's lap. Stacio knew for sure when he spotted Grandpa standing next to Michael with a hand on his shoulder. *My boy.*

Patty adjusted himself carefully on his stool, he was bruised and battered, wincing every time he drew a breath. Against his team's advice, Patty refused water and took another large gulp of cognac.

"You're fighting like a damn girl," Kenny yelled.

"He's throwing bricks at me. I never been hit so hard in my life," said Patty. "I think all my ribs are broken. He's gotta have something in his gloves."

Kenny grabbed Nellie and said, "Check his gloves."

Nellie hopped up on the side of the ring and waved O'Sullivan over. "I want a glove inspection," he said. "This guy's got plaster of Paris under there, I know it."

O'Sullivan walked up to Stacio and reached for his gloves. Stacio abided. "I'm sorry, Iceman," he said, and the crowd began to stir.

"What is this?" Father Henry asked the ref. "You know they're just buying time."

"I gotta check upon request, Father, I'm sorry," he said, pressing his thumbs into each of Stacio's knuckles.

O'Sullivan leaned over the ropes and yelled out to the judges, "He's clean."

When the bell finally rang, the crowd erupted again. Patty was so slow to get up that Stacio hit him before his stool was out of the ring. Patty fell back into his corner and Stacio viciously tenderized his body. Every single blow had brutal intentions. Even then, if Patty were to apologize for hurting Michael, Stacio would've dropped his gloves and left the stadium. But if given no other choice, he'd already decided that he would beat Patty to death.

"Apologize." Stacio yelled, landing another right hook that cracked two more of Patty's ribs.

"Never." Patty yelled back, clinging onto Stacio and headbutting him above the right eye.

The headbutt left Stacio with a nasty gash. He stumbled away and held his forehead, looking down at his blood dripping into the snow. Stacio looked back up at Patty, infuriated, but just before he charged at him the ref intervened.

"Timeout," O'Sullivan said, grabbing Stacio by the shoulders. "Are you all right?"

Stacio nodded his head. "I'm fine. Let us fight."

The entire crowd booed Patty and then began to chant, "The Champ is a chump. The Champ is a chump. The Champ is a chump."

O'Sullivan leaned over the rope to the judges. "O'Banion forfeits the round for his second violation," he said, holding up two fingers and glaring at Patty.

"Let me know when you're ready to go," said O'Sullivan, checking Stacio's cut.

"Now," he said, nudging the ref out of his way.

"Time in," said O'Sullivan, pointing at the judges before sliding away from the fighters.

Stacio stomped across the ring and cocked his right hand back. Patty tucked his arms in tight to protect his battered ribs. Stacio lunged forward and hit Patty square in the face. Patty took two steps back and fell flat on his ass. The entire ring shook when he hit the mat, but before O'Sullivan could start a count, the bell rang.

Patty held his head and spit out a mouthful of blood. He tried to adjust his broken nose, but his boxing gloves were too bulky. Nellie helped Patty up and guided him to the corner. Kenny threw the mink robe over him and dabbed his face with a rag. Nellie leaned in quick and reset Patty's busted nose. The sound always made Kenny cringe, so he turned away and covered his ears.

"Holy shit," Patty cried. "How about a little warning next time."

"He's killing you, Champ. Jab him," said Nellie. "Jab him and circle around."

"You want me to circle, huh?" Patty asked. "I can't even feel my damn feet, Nellie."

"You're the heavyweight champion of the world, Patty. Stick this bum. Jab him and move around." Nellie demanded.

Patty looked down at himself, his arms were black and blue, and his ribs were red, swollen, and covered in welts. The Champ had nothing left. He caught himself contemplating the towel for a split second, a very short, split second, but there was no doubt that it crossed his mind.

Never, he thought, *I'd rather die right here in this frozen hell.*

"Patty, you're gonna get yourself killed out there," said Kenny.

"I'm just so damn cold," he said. "I need a little more cognac."

"Sorry, Champ, you cleaned me out," Richie yelled from the ground. "Bone dry," he said, tipping the empty bottle upside down.

Patty had a coughing fit that ended with him spitting a wad of blood onto the canvas.

"Was that from your nose or your lungs?" Kenny asked.

"I don't know," said Patty. "I think it's a little bit of both."

"Nellie, we gotta throw the towel," Kenny said. "I think he's got a punctured lung or something."

"I agree," said Nellie, "but where the hell's Marty at?" He stood on his tippy toes and looked around the park. "This thing is definitely over with."

Patty stood up from his stool and grabbed Nellie by the shirt. "If you ever even think about throwing the towel in on me, I'll have your nuts tied to the back of my Duesenberg." Patty shoved Nellie toward the ropes and pointed at Kenny. "I ain't kidding, Kenny. You guys let me die in here before you ever throw any towel. O'Banion's don't know nuttin about throwing no towel."

Kenny raised both of his hands, shaking his head as he walked away.

Patty kicked his stool out of the ring and pointed a glove at Nellie. "I owe a lot to you, Nellie, but if I ever hear that come out of your mouth again, I will fire your ass."

Nellie nodded. "Sorry, Champ, just put this guy to sleep already, would ya?"

Jimmy packed a snowball and placed it on Stacio's cut. "It's not that bad, Stash, the bleeding already stopped."

"He's pulling every dirty trick in the book," Father Henry said. "I know you're tired, but he's hurt. Keep on pushing, brother, it's almost over."

Stacio nodded, then just as Jimmy fed him his mouthpiece, the bell rang.

Ubano rolled his window all the way down and pointed into the crowd. "Look who it is," he said. "The man of the hour."

Denny Lewis stood behind the judges, covering one eye with his scarf and praying for a victory. "Dear, Lord, let the Iceman finish him. Please!" he shouted.

Stacio marched across the ring like he was on fresh legs. Patty was wobbly, almost too tired and sore to lift his arms at all. Stacio shot in and continued to work the body. Patty just backpedaled and tried to avoid getting pinned in a corner. He dropped his arms all the way to his sides, desperate to protect his aching ribs. Stacio saw an opening and attacked. He swung a wild punch, aiming to take Patty's head clean off his shoulders. Unfortunately for him, the Champ was playing possum. It was a well placed trap, and the Iceman walked right into it.

Patty ducked under the punch and uppercut Stacio right in the groin. Stacio fell to his knees and wailed, holding his crotch with both gloves. Patty popped up and hit Stacio with a powerful right cross to the top of the head. Stacio collapsed to the canvas, his eyes were closed and his body was limp. The stadium got so quiet you could've heard a pin drop.

Grandpa's hand involuntarily clutched Michael's shoulder when Stacio went down.

Michael peeked over his blanket. "Ouch," he said, leaning away from his Grandfather's deadly embrace. "Don't squeeze me so hard."

"Oh, I'm sorry, Michael," he said, barely acknowledging his grandson as his eyes remained shackled to the ring. *Get up, Stacio. Get up.*

"Is Papa all right?" Michael asked, turning back to Grandpa. "That was a cheap shot, wasn't it?"

"Yeah, that was some cheap shot all right."

"Papa's tough," said Michael. "He'll get up."

"He will get up," said Grandpa. "Your father is very tough."

Grandpa clenched his jaw and furrowed his brow. *Dirty, Irish, cheating bastard. I oughta put my shotgun right under your chin*, he yelled, but only in his own head.

"Get up, son… Get up," Grandpa grunted under his breath, squeezing Michael's shoulder again.

"Get up, Papa." Michael yelled, placing his hand over Grandpa's and yanking his shoulder free.

All of the air came out of a confident Denny Lewis the instant

Stacio hit the mat. Denny closed his eyes and slumped his shoulders, a common mannerism he'd display just before losing any bet. Before Denny could do anything, Ubano's men moved in behind him.

"The Boss wants you to come sit in the car with us," said Franky, planting a firm hand on Denny's upper back. "Come on, Screw, the Lincoln's nice and toasty."

Stacio was semi-conscious, he tried to get up, but his body wasn't cooperating. He rolled around on the canvas, dazed and helpless.

"Start the count already," Richie yelled from his brother's corner.

O'Sullivan pushed Patty away from the Iceman. "Get back, O'Banion. That was another cheap shot."

"Get up, brother. Get up," Father Henry yelled into the ring.

Patty shoved O'Sullivan backwards. "It was an honest mistake, ref. I swear," he said. "Just go count this bozo out already."

O'Sullivan shoved Patty back into the ropes, delaying the count even longer. "Don't you ever put your hands on me, O'Banion."

"Sorry, sorry," said Patty, raising his hands and stepping back. "Just go do your little count and let's get outta here."

Patty turned to the crowd and raised his gloves in victory. He looked shocked when the entire stadium began to boo.

"Ah, who needs ya," he said, rolling his eyes and waving them off.

"One," O'Sullivan began the count. "Two... Three..."

Stacio rolled onto his side and shook his head, struggling to compose himself. He forced his eyes open and searched the crowd for Michael. Time seemed to be standing still, and everything was muffled except for his own breathing. Deep breaths echoed through Stacio's mind, and what felt like an eternity laying there looking for his son, was mere seconds. When his eyes finally found Michael, everything went black.

Stacio saw himself holding Michael for the very first time at a run-down hospital on the Southside of Chicago. Michael was so small, swaddled in a blue receiving blanket with a baby blue hat sitting loose on his tiny head. Stacio gazed at his newborn son, overflowing with joy and gratitude. He looked up at Linda and said, "He's perfect."

Next, Stacio saw himself come into the house after a hard day of working in the summer heat. He set down his thermos and walked into the kitchen, where Linda was feeding Michael in his highchair.

Michael peeked around his mother and looked right into Stacio's eyes. He couldn't have been more than eight months old. "Dada," he said, pointing his chubby, little finger directly at his father.

That was one of the happiest memories of Stacio's entire life. Still, to this day, he remembered the way his heart flipped in his chest when Michael said his first word.

"Four... Five," O'Sullivan's voice crept into the memory.

Stacio's eyes opened to find Michael in the White Sox dugout. He couldn't hear anything, but he could read his son's lips, "Get up, Papa. Get up."

Stacio's eyes closed again, and another memory began to play in his mind. Michael was crawling all over the place and getting into everything. Linda was upstairs hiding Christmas gifts, while Grandpa was handling the two older boys in the backyard. Stacio was hovering over Michael, keeping him out of the garbage, the dog food, and the kitchen cabinets. Michael grabbed onto a chair and pulled himself up to his feet. Stacio moved in close to protect his head if he fell, but Michael looked sturdy. Stacio took a step back and crouched down, admiring his son.

Michael turned himself around, then he reached out his hands and walked. Stacio scooted back slowly, holding his hands out a few

feet in front of his son. By the time Michael reached his father, he'd

walked almost ten feet. Those were Michael's first steps, and it was

another memory Stacio held dear to his heart. It was a special

moment this father and son would share until the end of time, no

matter what. Michael was too small to remember, but it was

something Stacio could never forget. Just then, the thought of a baby

Michael taking his first steps across the kitchen was interrupted.

Stacio was startled as every car in the stadium started honking

and flashing their high-beams. One of the headlights caught the

metal frame on Michael's wheelchair and reflected into Stacio's

eyes, snapping him back to reality.

My boy walked, he thought. *My boy walked, but he'll never walk*

again. That terrible truth pumped fury through Stacio's veins. He

clenched his fists as his crystal blue eyes exploded open.

He grabbed onto O'Sullivan's pant leg and pulled himself half

way up before slipping.

"Six… Seven," O'Sullivan continued his count.

Stacio grabbed his leg again and pulled himself up, using

O'Sullivan's coat for balance.

Patty looked over at Nellie and said, "Hey, he can't do that."

Nellie hopped up on the side of the ring and yelled, "Hey, ref, that's not allowed."

O'Sullivan pulled his coat free and Stacio stayed up. O'Sullivan walked over and stood in front of Nellie. "You wanna talk to me about the rules?" he asked. "You're lucky he's not disqualified. That was a blatant low-blow, and a fourth cheap shot. Four dirty moves from a dirty fighter. He's supposed to be the class of boxing, a champion for crying out loud." O'Sullivan glared over at Patty. "It's a disgrace. You should all be embarrassed," he said, making his way back to the center of the ring. He held up a finger and looked at Patty. "One more, O'Banion. One more and you forfeit the match. I'm not kidding. Keep it clean and let's finish this fight, men."

Nellie hopped off the ring and looked at Kenny. "He's right, Kenny, this isn't what we're about."

"I know it ain't," he said. "I just wanna get him the hell out of there."

When O'Sullivan said, 'Fight', and slid out of the way, the crowd went wild. Within seconds, every single person in the arena was chanting, "Ice-man. Ice-man. Ice-man."

Patty looked around the stadium, disgusted and defeated. He turned to his corner and shook his head.

"Knock this guy out," said Nellie. "It's the only thing you can do now, but you gotta do it clean."

Patty nodded his head and turned to face Stacio. The Iceman had a crazed look in his eyes, his stone cold glare locked in on the Champ. Something was different now, something had changed. The Iceman had become the hunter, his focus was unnerving. He stared through Patty the way a lion would stare through a gazelle just before it pounced. The two men were no longer opponents, Stacio was a predator, and Patty was his prey. The Iceman clenched his fists, licked his chops, and moved in for the kill.

The Champ backed into a corner and tried to guard as much of himself as he could. He peeked through his gloves, but all he could see was snow whipping around in the darkness. Headlights reflected off of the white streams, creating the illusion of ghosts dancing around the ring. Patty rubbed his eyes and squinted through the swirls, bracing himself for impact. Like lightning, the Iceman appeared through the drift and pounded Patty's ribs. Patty hunched over and lost his mouthpiece. Stacio hit him again, and again, and again, beating the Champ all the way down to his knees. The bell rang and Stacio hit him one last time before O'Sullivan pulled him back and walked him toward his corner.

Richie and Kenny hopped in the ring. They lifted Patty to his feet and set him down softly on his stool.

"Did you see that beating?" Denny asked, getting sandwiched between Ubano and Lou in the back of the warm Lincoln. Franky hopped in the front seat with Vito and turned to face the back. Denny looked nervous, rubbing his hands together to warm them up.

"I can feel the wind coming off of you," said Ubano. "It's cold out there, huh?"

"Colder than a polar bear's ballsack," said Denny, making the entire car laugh. "I've never seen anything like this."

"You and me both," said Franky.

Ubano reached into his pocket and Denny leaned away, hoping it wasn't a pistol. "Relax, Screw, If I was gonna give you the long nap, I wouldn't do it in my favorite Lincoln."

Denny laughed nervously.

"Here, this belongs to you," said Ubano, handing him the Silver Star.

"Fight's not over," he said.

"It's over," said Ubano. "The Champ threw everything at him. He used every dirty trick in the book, but your Iceman's still standing. O'Banion's got nothing left. This was never really even a fight."

Denny took the Silver Star from Ubano and spun it between his finger and thumb, smiling.

"Maybe the Champ can hit him with that obnoxious belt of his," said Franky. "Irish bum loses me money fighting a nobody. This is ridiculous."

"I told you not to bet against the Iceman," said Lou. "A baseball bat couldn't put this guy down."

Franky mumbled more Italian curses under his breath.

"You were right," said Ubano, "your Iceman is one tough Polak. And thanks to you, I put a grand on him."

Denny's mouth dropped. "A grand?"

"A grand," said Ubano, shaking Denny by the shoulders and laughing. "A thousand dollars! You talked me into it, you crazy bastard."

"I put five hundred on him myself," said Lou. "All that Iceman talk got me to remembering how tough my old man's father was. It takes a certain kind of strength to do a job like that every day"

Denny looked around the car and let out a sigh of relief. When Ubano's men brought him to the Lincoln, he thought the Town Car might be his coffin. Never in a million years did he expect it to be a victory party, all dedicated to the man they called 'Screwloose'. Denny wasn't used to winning, but with his life on the line, he needed this one more than ever.

"Hey, Franky, tell Denny how much dough the Iceman made you tonight," said Lou, poking Franky in the back of the shoulder.

"I don't wanna talk about it," he said, smacking Lou's hand away.

"Thirty years I've known this guy," said Ubano, pointing a thumb at Franky. "He's never liked ice. Never seen him use it, not even once."

"I told you, Boss, I got sensitive teeth," he said.

"Always been a sore loser, too," Ubano whispered.

Franky rolled his eyes while the rest of the men laughed.

Patty sat on his stool, barely able to stay upright. Kenny threw the mink robe over his brother and began pleading with him, "We have to get you out of here, Patty. Now," he said. "Just let him throw the towel, who gives a shit."

Patty shook his head. "No," he grunted, looking over his shoulder toward the White Sox dugout. His eyes scanned the area until they found Michael. Patty focused in and examined the boy in his wheelchair. *I didn't see ya, kid. If I saw ya, I would've swerved the other way,* Patty thought. *I feel pretty bad for ya. I probably don't feel as bad as I should, and there's no way in hell that I'd switch places with ya, but I'm no monster. I didn't mean to hurt ya, kid. I swear it.*

Kenny grabbed Patty's ear, snapping him back to reality. "You told the priest that 'it would be a cold day in hell' before you apologized. Look around, Patty, hell's frozen over. Apologize to this lunatic and let's get you to a hospital."

Patty shook his head again. "No," he said, coughing blood down the front of his mink robe.

"Jesus, look at you," said Kenny, balling up a handful of Patty's robe to wipe the blood away from his mouth.

Patty leaned around Kenny and fixed his eyes on Michael. "It was an accident," he said.

"I know it was an accident, Patty. Just say you're sorry to the Iceman and let's get the hell out of here," said Kenny. "That's all he wants."

"I won't quit," Patty said, nudging Kenny out of his way to see Stacio. "O'Banion's never quit nuttin."

Stacio stood with his back to Patty, he leaned on the ropes and listened to his brother. "Don't give him any more chances. He's a dirty fighter," said Father Henry. "End this immediately. Do you hear me, Stacio?"

Stacio removed his mouthpiece, he looked intensely into his brother's eyes and said, "I'll put my fist through him."

Father Henry nodded his head and then looked at Jimmy.

Jimmy raised his eyebrows and said, "That was scary."

"Yeah, and he meant it," said Father Henry.

When the bell rang, Stacio glided through the heavy snow like a phantom, disappearing and reappearing in front of Patty almost instantly. Patty was startled by how fast the Iceman moved. Stacio hit him with a heavy right hook to the ribs, folding Patty over and launching him back into his corner. Patty braced his body against the ropes and tried desperately to defend himself. Stacio just pummeled him with relentless punches to the body. Patty yelped every time a fist landed on him, his face distorted by the crippling pain. He clung to Stacio with everything he had left, trying to get a break from the onslaught.

Before O'Sullivan moved in to pry them apart, Stacio shoved Patty against the ropes, beating him like a speed bag each time he sprung back. Patty hunched over and shielded his body, coughing up more blood and spitting it onto the icy canvas. O'Sullivan pulled Stacio back and took a knee next to Patty. "If you don't fight back, I gotta call it," he said.

"Don't you dare," said Patty, hopping up and shoving the ref out of the way.

Stacio moved in strategically, taking short steps to let his opponent come to him. Patty lunged in, throwing sloppy punches all over the place. The pain he felt from hitting empty air was enough to make most men quit, but like the Champ said, 'O'Banion's never quit nuttin'. Patty gathered every single drop he had left in the tank as he cocked back and threw the mother of all bombs. It was fast, it was heavy, and it was on its way to put the Iceman to sleep for good. The punch was so powerful the judges could feel the velocity from outside of the ring.

Stacio leaned back and turned his head, Patty's glove just grazing the tip of his nose. The Champ swung so hard that his momentum almost threw him flat on his face. He fell to one knee and planted his left glove on the ground, leaving his ribcage fully exposed. The Iceman shot in and blasted Patty's body with a savage right hook. Everyone within fifteen feet of the impact could hear Patty's ribs snap like a bundle of sticks. The Champ went down on all fours, coughing blood all over himself and the ring. O'Sullivan shoved Stacio back to his corner and ran to Patty's side.

Stacio stood with his arms out to his sides. "Just apologize," he begged.

Patty shook his head and spit up more blood.

"You crippled my boy, O'Banion," Stacio pleaded. "Just apologize. Aren't you sorry?"

The bell rang and Patty's brothers rushed to his side. Father Henry climbed into the ring and pulled Stacio back to his corner.

"Jesus Christ," Kenny cried, trying to pull Patty up. "Get his other arm, Richie."

Patty howled out in excruciating pain when they lifted him to the stool.

Father Henry reached his hand over the ropes. "Give me the water, Jimmy."

Jimmy held the water bottle upside down and shook his head. "It's frozen, Father."

Father Henry bent over and packed a snowball. He held it up to Stacio's mouth and said, "Eat this. You haven't had nearly enough water for this kind of fight."

"Why won't he say it?" Stacio asked, guiding the snowball away from his face. "Why won't he just say it?"

"I don't know, maybe he's just too hard-headed," said Father Henry, turning to glance at Patty's corner. Nellie, O'Sullivan, and Patty's brothers were all huddled around him in a panic. "He's human, though, and I'd be willing to bet he's been sorry from the start."

"I can't breathe," said Patty, clutching onto Richie's shirt.

"Do something," Richie cried, shaking Kenny by the shoulder.

"We need an ambulance," Nellie screamed out toward the judges.

Kenny stood in front of Patty and held him by the shoulders. "Don't die on me," he begged, drying tears from his cheeks with both hands. "We're gonna get you to a hospital."

"No," Patty said with a soft, wheezy breath.

"He's done. This is done," said Richie.

Kenny turned toward Nellie. "Throw the towel, it's over."

Nellie waved the white towel and one of the judges rang the bell. The frozen crowd cheered.

Stacio walked slowly to the center of the ring. "This isn't over," he mumbled.

Father Henry looked up at the sky and smiled. Jimmy hopped into the ring and tried to guide Stacio back to his corner.

"But, it's not over," said Stacio, wiggling free before kneeling in the center of the ring.

Jimmy turned to look at Father Henry, holding his arms out to his sides. "I'm not gonna drag him," he said. "He's too damn strong."

"He's fine," said Father Henry, waving Jimmy back. "Just leave him be."

Nellie squeezed between the brothers and covered Patty with the soiled, mink robe. Barely any traces of white were left as blood seeped through the fabric and coated most of the fur. Patty was too sore to do it himself, so Richie wrapped the robe around him.

"Easy," Patty begged, clenching his teeth.

He reached out slowly, spreading his brothers apart to look across the ring at Stacio.

"Apologize," Stacio begged, holding his gloves together as if praying. "Apologize for what you did to my boy. Please."

Patty hung his head for a moment, wincing at every movement he made. He pulled Kenny down to him and whispered something in his ear. Nellie pried the ropes open as much as he could, while Kenny and Richie lifted Patty out of the ring. The crowd began to cheer again, prompting Patty's entire team to stop and look back.

O'Sullivan was in the middle of the ring with Stacio, raising the Iceman's glove for all to see, declaring him the victor of one of the hardest fought battles in boxing history.

The hardest fight of my entire life, Patty thought, removing his arm from around Richie to whisper something to his team. Patty motioned Nellie to come take Richie's place under his arm for support, then Kenny nodded in approval to whatever Patty had told Richie to do.

Richie walked back and tossed the heavyweight championship belt into the ring. The belt slid across the slushy surface and stopped at O'Sullivan's feet. He bent down and picked it up, then he pulled a small white towel from his waistband. He dried the belt from strap to strap, then he presented it to Stacio. The Iceman looked at it for a moment, and then he looked back to the crowd to find his son. Michael had the biggest smile on his face, cheering and swinging his scarf above his head like a helicopter.

Stacio reached out and took the belt. He ran his fingers along the leather and over its golden face. Even then, he couldn't believe what was in his hands.

"Raise it, Iceman," said O'Sullivan, "you certainly earned it."

When Stacio raised the championship belt the crowd exploded into cheers. It was so loud the ref had to hold his hands over his earmuffs. Rumor has it, you could hear them cheering all the way from Michigan that night. People were laying on their car horns so long they burnt them out. People pounded their feet so hard that a section of the bleachers collapsed. People screamed so long, and so loud that they fainted and woke up covered in snow. It was insane, the entire place was out of control. Stacio dropped his arm, letting the belt hang limp against his side. He watched closely as Patty made a beeline for the White Sox dugout.

"The kid," said Patty, staggering toward Michael with the help of his team.

Grandpa put his hand in his pocket to feel for his pistol. Michael rewrapped his scarf and peered over it, looking up at a conquered Patty O'Banion. The wind was howling, nearly blowing Patty over when he took his arms off of Kenny and Nellie.

"Let me stand," he said, hobbling to get directly in front of Michael. "Kid... I'm... I just want to say... Ahh."

Patty leaned away from Michael and coughed a wad of blood into the snow. Kenny reached out and tried to help Patty get upright, but he pushed Kenny's hands away and stood on his own. Patty turned and looked back into the ring. Stacio dropped the belt and held his gloves together, urging Patty to speak.

Patty turned back to Michael and said, "Listen, Kid, I just wanna say... Ahh." Patty dropped to one knee and coughed up another wad of blood. He was wheezing hard and gurgling too much blood to speak. He let Kenny help him back to his feet, then he leaned in close to Michael.

Grandpa cocked the pistol in his pocket and moved closer to his grandson. Stacio locked eyes with Grandpa and nodded his head in approval, prompting him to take his hand off of his gun.

Patty grimaced as he reached out to Michael, everything hurting. He patted Michael on the head gently, leaving him with a crooked hat. Michael looked up at Patty with a faint smile on his face. Patty smiled back, then he turned toward the ring. He nodded at Stacio and the Iceman nodded back, the standoff was finally over and both men felt a sense of relief. Patty hobbled toward the dark tunnel with one brother under each arm, his mink robe leaving a trail of blood in the snow behind them.

"I can't believe I won. I can't believe I really won," said Denny. "I never win... Ever."

"Put the money in the bank, Denny. Buy some bonds or something," said Ubano. "You place another bet and I'll kill you myself. As of today, your betting days are over."

"Buy a house and settle down," said Franky. "Get out of that dump you stay at."

"I got a bet for ya," said Vito. "I bet dollars to donuts that this loser blows that money in a week."

Ubano leaned forward and smacked the driver in the back of the head.

"Jesus," said Vito, fixing his hat.

"Anybody calls this man a loser and they have to deal with me," said Ubano. "He's got a Silver Star for crying out loud. Show some respect."

"I was kidding around, Boss," said Vito. "I'm sorry."

Ubano grabbed the Silver Star and pinned it to Denny's coat. "From now on, Screw, you're golden," he said.

"Thanks, I appreciate that," said Denny.

"No, thank you," said Ubano.

"Hey, not that I mind it, but I gotta ask," Denny said. "Why've you always been so good to me? Anyone else in holes like mine and they'd get the cement shoes, no question."

Ubano looked at Denny and took a deep breath. "I ain't getting too much into it, but I'll tell you that I grew up an Army brat," he said, pointing to the medal on Denny's coat. "And something like that means something to me. I never like to hurt a veteran, so I do everything I can to avoid it."

"That's it?" Denny asked.

"Yeah," said Ubano. "That's it."

"Jeez," said Denny, putting a hand on Ubano's shoulder. "If I'd have known, maybe I would've dug a little deeper."

All five men laughed for a moment, until Ubano put a hand on Denny's shoulder and said, "I know you got a few screws loose, my friend, but don't press your luck. You were damn close to swimming with the fishes."

"Hey, all joking aside," said Denny, "you're a good man, Ubano."

Denny held out his hand. Ubano reached out and shook it. "Likewise," he said, tapping the driver on the shoulder. "Hey, Vito, why don't you get us outta here, I could use a cappuccino."

"You got it, Boss," said Vito, shifting the Lincoln into drive and pulling out.

Workers were in the ring shoveling the canvas and chipping ice off the turnbuckles. They were attempting to get everything ready for disassemblement, but the blizzard had other plans. Stacio just stood motionless in the center of the ring, staring down at the slush-covered championship belt.

One after another, all the cars exited the stadium in a neat line. Everybody rushed out of the park to find someplace warm, even the drunkest revelers were too frozen to celebrate. Within minutes, the entire stadium cleared out. Even the men who were responsible for breaking down the ring surrendered to the cold and left. Father Henry and Jimmy walked up and stood on each side of Stacio.

"It's time to go," said Father Henry. "We've done our job well. You especially."

"Yeah," said Jimmy, "we gotta get you outta this cold."

Stacio looked up at them. "Thank you both for everything," he said, "but you can go, I'll be fine."

"Stacio." Father Henry thought to argue.

"Go," he said, more stern the second time. "I need to be alone."

Father Henry looked at his brother and nodded, Stacio nodded back.

Jimmy grabbed Stacio by the shoulder as he walked past him. "No matter what happens next," said Jimmy, "you're a hero. Don't forget that, Iceman."

Stacio locked eyes with Jimmy and gave him a firm pat on the back. "Thank you," he said.

The two men exited the ring and disappeared up the tunnel, leaving Stacio all alone in the solitary stadium. Once Father Henry and Jimmy were gone, the Iceman fell to his knees and slammed his gloves to the canvas. He closed his eyes and sat there in the dark, as still as a statue, a statue in the middle of an ice cold, swirling blizzard.

Chapter Thirty-one

The heavy weight of victory

Stacio sat motionless in him armchair, facing the fireplace with his eyes clamped shut. A fire roared in front of him, spreading warm waves across his face and chest. His fingers hung loose over the edge of the armrests, his hands still taped up from the fight. The tape was worn out on the knuckles, but still clinging strong to his hands and wrists. His soaking wet boots were propped up on a log in front of him, and his bare feet had small puddles around them. Stacio's chest rose and fell hard as he inhaled deep breaths of warmth.

Grandpa was sitting with his eyes closed, too, rocking next to his radio just outside the doorway of the family room. He sprung forward and opened his eyes, turning up the volume before leaning in close to the speaker. A few moments later, Grandpa stood up and shuffled to the doorway. "Stacio," he said. "On the radio… they say O'Banion is dead."

Stacio never opened his eyes, but his hands gripped the armrests so tight that the wood almost crumbled. He took another deep breath and his hands relaxed, the wood creaking as the pressure lessened.

Grandpa just stood there, helpless. "I'm here if you need me, son."

Stacio said nothing, he only sat there soaking up the warmth and resting his tired body. Grandpa frowned, realizing there was nothing he could do or say to help. He stared at his son for a few more seconds before limping back to his rocking chair.

The next day, Grandpa sat at the kitchen table sipping his coffee. Linda stood at the stove stirring a pot of chicken noodle soup.

"He's been sitting in that chair for days," she said. "I'm really worried about him. This is not like Stacio."

"He went through hell, Linda," Grandpa said. "You didn't see it. It's unexplainable. Just give him a little more time."

"Fine, but he absolutely has to eat this soup," she said. "I will not take 'no' for an answer."

"I'll plug his nose and you shove the spoon in," Grandpa whispered, laughing under his breath.

Linda's mouth only turned up faintly on the ends, but it was the closest thing to a smile she'd delivered in days.

"That's better," said Grandpa. "This house is too gloomy when you're not smiling."

Before Linda could respond, the doorbell rang and the dog barked. "Oh, hush," she said, shooing the dog away from the front door. "Go lay down."

Linda opened the door and saw Molly standing on the porch. She was wearing a long black dress with a fancy black hat. She had on black satin gloves with a black handkerchief clutched in her right hand. A black veil covered her face, but it wasn't enough to hide her swollen eyes.

"Come here, sweetie," said Linda, wrapping her arms around Molly and squeezing her tight. "I'm so sorry for your loss."

Stacio was still sitting motionless in his armchair, but his eyes were wide open, staring hard into the fire. Linda came through the threshold, followed by Molly. Stacio didn't even notice them, he was fixated on the flames, lost somewhere in his own head.

"He's been sitting here like this since the fight," said Linda. "He hasn't eaten, showered, or spoken to anyone."

Molly took a few steps closer to Stacio. "My husband is dead," she said. "I just came here to say a few things. You never knew Patrick the way that I knew him. He was just a big kid. A big, stubborn, but lovable kid. I know the way that he handled Michael's accident was disgraceful and disgusting, but it really was an accident. Patrick could be cocky, vain, and very rough around the edges, but he would never intentionally hurt a child. He loved children. Patty always wanted to be a father." Molly had to stop for a moment to fight back tears. She took a deep breath, cleared her throat and continued, "I don't blame you, Stacio, not one bit. You fought for what was right, everyone knows it. I just hope that you weren't expecting my husband's death to bring you peace, because an eye for an eye only makes the whole world blind."

Stacio's gaze broke away from the fire and found Molly. "Peace? How could this bring me peace?" he asked. "My son is still crippled, and now you're a widow," he said, clutching the armrests again. "This was never my intention. Something very bad happened to my boy, and the way that it was handled was criminal. I had to do something, because no one else was going to do anything. Sometimes an eye for an eye is a father's only choice."

Molly looked down and dabbed her cheeks with her

handkerchief.

Stacio scooted to the edge of his seat and found Molly's eyes through her veil. "If Michael was your child," he said, "would you have just let it go?"

Molly stood up straight and cleared her throat, "Absolutely not," she said. "The service is tomorrow... Do whatever's in your heart."

Molly reached out and grabbed Linda's hand. "Thank you for everything," she whispered, squeezing and letting go before hurrying out the front door.

After a few minutes of silence, Stacio groaned when he stood up to stretch his stiff back. Linda and Grandpa glanced at each other before rushing over to peek into the room. Stacio was standing in front of the fireplace, struggling to free himself from the ragged tape left on his fists. His hands were so battered he couldn't even tear back a frayed strip to get started.

"Here," said Linda. "Let me."

She came into the room with scissors and carefully cut him free, revealing his black-and-blue fists. He held his palm out and reached for the wad of tape in Linda's hand. She looked at him funny. "You want this," she asked, handing it to him when he nodded his head.

"Thank you," he said, turning back to the fireplace.

Stacio looked down at the tattered nest and took a deep breath. He tossed it into the fire and clenched his jaw as he watched it burn. Grandpa and Linda just stood there in silence, waiting to see what he would do next.

"What time is it?" he asked.

Grandpa flipped his pocket watch open and said, "Almost noon."

"And what day?"

"It's Tuesday," said Linda, placing a loving hand on the back of his shoulder. "You haven't moved in days."

Grandpa stepped forward to get a better look at Stacio's hands. "The last thing you probably wanna feel is cold," he said, "but you really oughta ice those hands, son."

"Thanks, Pop, but I'm fine," said Stacio, bending down and grabbing his work boots.

"I made soup," said Linda. "Why don't you come to the table and have a bowl. It's chicken noodle, your favorite."

"I have to go to the icehouse," he said. "I'll have my soup right when I get back. I promise."

"Degan knows what ya been through, Stacio, he was at the fight," said Grandpa. "He told me to let you rest as long as you need. You should have a little soup before you go."

"I won't be long," said Stacio, kissing Linda on the forehead before walking out of the room.

Chapter Thirty-two

Two days in twenty-something years

Stacio trotted Chestnut to the front door of Degan's Icehouse. He pulled back gently on her reins, wincing at the pain in his hands. He grabbed a bag off the seat next to him and hid it in the bed of the carriage. He looked around to make sure nobody saw him before he slammed the tailgate shut.

"I'll be right back, girl," he said, carefully sliding his fingers over her mane as he went by.

Stacio walked inside and made his first left into Degan's office. The phone rang and a silver haired man in overalls lifted it to his ear. "Degan speaking," he said, looking up and smiling at the sight of Stacio. "Please, give us a few days, everyone's gonna get their ice. Thank you for your patience."

Degan set the phone down and stood up from his chair. He was a weathered, old man with an anchor tattoo on his forearm.

"How ya doing, Stash," he asked, barely getting the words out before the phone rang again. Shaking his head, Degan turned the phone upside down and disconnected the chord. "Problem solved," he laughed. "You all right? That was some fight."

"I'm fine, thank you," said Stacio. "I just wanted to come and apologize for not being here. I'll be in tomorrow, and I'll have everything back in order by Friday."

"Apologize? You kidding me," Degan said, patting Stacio on the shoulder. "You missed what, two days in twenty-something years. This place would've been shut down and long gone a decade ago if it wasn't for you carrying it on your back. Don't be crazy, Stash, you come to work whenever you're ready."

"I'm ready."

"Good," said Degan, pointing back at the phone, "cause that damn thing hasn't stopped ringing since the fight. Everybody and their mothers are calling here looking for you."

"Looking for me? Why," Stacio asked. "What do they want from me?"

"They want your ice, Stacio. Nobody in Chicago wants any other ice anymore, they only want yours."

"But my ice is the same as all the other ice."

"Not anymore," said Degan.

Later that afternoon, Stacio and Chestnut strolled into Northside Chicago without a single block of ice for sale. They were headed to Patty's Place when two young, Irish cops spotted them at a busy intersection. *Here we go,* Stacio thought to himself, clutching onto the bag in his passenger seat. To his surprise, the cops got out of their vehicle and stopped traffic to let him cross. Stacio nodded as he went by and both cops tipped their caps respectfully.

"Good afternoon, Iceman," one of them said.

"Good afternoon to you," Stacio replied.

A few blocks from Patty's Place at one of the nicest buildings in the neighborhood, Stacio saw Denny Lewis walk into the vestibule with a key in his hand and a briefcase under his arm. Denny was clean-cut and sober, coming home from work to his brand new pad. Stacio smiled and thought, *Good for him.*

Chestnut stopped near the front entrance of Patty's Place, but all the lights were out and the 'Closed' sign was hanging in the new storefront window. Stacio reached into the bag and pulled out the heavyweight championship belt. He blew hot air on its golden face and buffed out the smudges with his sleeve before sliding it back into the bag. Just as he lifted Chestnut's reins, two men walked up from different directions.

"Hey, Stash, I need a delivery tomorrow morning," said one of the men.

"Take me first, Iceman, I got a pizza pie in the oven," said the other.

Stacio pulled out his notepad. "One at a time, please," he said, nodding at the pizza man.

"Right behind Patty's Place to the left," said the pizza man, pointing in the direction he was talking about. "Rocco's Pizza, it's three doors over on the corner of Tillman Street."

"The corner of Tillman Street," Stacio repeated, jotting notes in his pad. "I know the place."

Chapter Thirty-three

Sad Violin

It was a cold, but sunny day at Chicago's Graceland Cemetery. Cops

and security guards held fans and media at bay just outside the

graveyard's stone walls. A modest gathering of mourners stood near

Patty's open grave. Bagpipes echoed along acres of snowy

headstones and neatly trimmed landscape. Molly wept with dignity,

dabbing her tears with a silky black handkerchief. Kenny and Richie

were a mess, fighting back their sadness as the priest began his

eulogy.

"Even though we walk through the valley of the shadow of death,

we shall fear no evil..."

Molly tapped a few shoulders, separating people to make room

for Linda, who was pushing Michael's wheelchair toward the front

row. Molly gave Michael a warm smile, and he smiled back. Linda

put a hand on Molly's shoulder. "I'm here for you," she whispered.

"Thank you," said Molly, covering her face with both hands.

"Come here, sweetie," said Linda, wrapping her arms around Molly. "Let it out."

Stacio and Grandpa stood alone, tucked between two rows of bushes almost fifty feet away from Patty's grave. Grandpa wore a spiffy black suit with a black and gray fedora. Stacio's suit was a bit worn out and a few sizes too small, but it was the only suit in his closet.

When Kenny realized Michael was there, he looked around to make sure the Iceman didn't show up. He nearly growled when he spotted them standing off to the side with their eyes closed and their heads bowed. His face hardened as anger surged through his veins. He bit his bottom lip and stomped toward Stacio. "What the hell is he doing here," he said, pushing his way through the crowd.

Richie grabbed onto him, trying his best to hold Kenny back, but he was too big and too strong to contain. "Please, Kenny, not here," he begged.

"Let go of my arm, Richie."

"Kenny, for God's sake, it's Patty's funeral."

"And whose fault is that, huh?" he asked, breaking loose and standing toe-to-toe with Stacio, hunching over more than a foot to look him in the eye. "This is a private ceremony," he grunted.

Stacio stepped back, he leaned over and reached into a bag on the ground beside him. He took out the championship belt and presented it to Kenny. "I wanted to return this," he said. "It belongs with the champion."

Kenny yanked it out of Stacio's hands and shoved it into Richie's chest. "I speak for all of us when I say you aren't welcome here."

"We were invited," said Stacio, staring at the ground.

Kenny looked over to Molly, who was crying on Linda's shoulder. "By her?" he asked. "We never really thought of her as family," he said, poking a finger into Stacio's chest as he spoke. "She's a Polak, just like you."

Kenny stepped closer to Stacio, towering over him. "You got a lot of nerve showing up here, Iceman," he said, twisting Stacio's shirt up with his big fists. Stacio stood motionless in Kenny's grasp, staring up at him with remorseful eyes.

Richie reached out and put a hand on his brother's shoulder. "That's enough, Kenny."

Kenny shrugged him away and started to lift Stacio off the

ground. "You killed him," he said. "You killed my little brother."

Stacio showed zero resistance, hanging in Kenny's massive arms like a ragdoll.

Grandpa walked up and grabbed Kenny's wrists. "Let him be," he said. "We've all got some forgiving to do."

Kenny dropped Stacio and loosened his grip. He looked at Grandpa and nodded. He closed his eyes and slumped his shoulders, then he took a deep breath and bowed his head.

Molly and Linda separated, standing on opposite sides of Michael's wheelchair. He placed one arm over each of their shoulders as they lifted him to his feet. He locked his leg braces into place and steadied himself before they let go. Molly took his violin out of its case and handed it to him. Linda and Molly stared in amazement at the resilient young man standing, not sitting, but standing in front of them. Michael tucked the violin under his chin and began to play.

Everything came to a halt when the piece, 'Sad Violin', began to sing like angels from Michael's strings. It was the most beautiful melody anyone had ever heard, uplifting and haunting at the same time. All of the mourners lifted their heads and gasped at the sight. A shock to everyone that this glorious sound was coming from this young boy. This young, crippled boy who was standing on his own two legs to celebrate the man who bound him to his chair. It was touching, it was overwhelming, and it was absolutely beautiful. If everyone could be like this boy, like Michael, the world would be a much more beautiful place.

If this isn't poetic, I don't know that anything is, Molly thought, staring proudly at her protégé.

Stacio lifted his head. "Michael," he mumbled. "That's... that's my boy."

Within seconds, there wasn't a dry eye left at the Graceland Cemetery. Kenny began to bawl. He let go of Stacio and patted him on the chest. "I'm sorry," he said, turning away to hug Richie.

The O'Banion brothers cried on one another's shoulder, it was the joyous release of emotion that everybody needed.

Grandpa put an arm around Stacio, tears rushing to their eyes as they stared through the crowd at Michael.

"That kid is something else," said Grandpa.

"I know it," said Stacio, drying his eyes on his collar. "I love that boy."

"You and me both," Grandpa said, blowing his nose into a gray handkerchief.

Richie leaned in and handed Stacio a long-stemmed rose. "You're a brave man," he said, "and a great fighter, too."

"Thank you," said Stacio, twirling the rose gently between his finger and thumb.

Kenny grabbed the championship belt from Richie's shoulder and walked toward Patty's grave. "Come on, Richie, it's time to say goodbye."

Richie, Grandpa, and Stacio all followed him as everyone lined up to pay their last respects.

When Michael finished playing, he sat in his chair and Linda wheeled him up to the edge of the grave. "I forgive you," he said, tossing a rose onto Patty's casket. "Rest in peace, Champ."

Linda smiled at her son and tossed in a rose of her own, followed by Grandpa.

Stacio stopped at the foot of the grave and looked down at the rose twirling between his fingers. *I'm sorry it had to end like this,* he thought. *It was a bumpy ride, but you ended up doing the right thing. Thank you for that.* Stacio dropped his rose on Patty's coffin and mumbled under his breath, "Rest in peace, Champion." He began to move along, but his head turned back when a hand touched him on the shoulder.

"Thank you for coming," Molly whispered.

"Of course," said Stacio. "I'm truly sorry for all of this."

"I know you are," she said, "but it's not your fault."

Stacio took a deep breath and nodded his head. "Take care of yourself," he said, placing a gentle hand on her shoulder before walking away.

Molly stood there for a moment, she dried her eyes, bowed her head, and began to pray. When she finished, she made the sign of the cross and looked up at the sky, tears pouring down her face. "I'll always love you, Patrick," she whispered, kissing her rose before dropping it onto his casket.

Richie walked up with his flask in hand, untwisting the cap with his teeth. He took two sips for himself before pouring some into the grave for his fallen brother. "You did real good for yourself, Champ. You brought a lot of pride to the O'Banion name." Richie rubbed his swollen eyes with the back of his hands and continued, "I'm gonna miss ya… but I'll see ya on the other side. Say hello to Ma and Pop for me, would ya?" Richie tossed his rose on top of Patty's coffin, taking another long sip from his flask as he walked away.

Kenny was the last one in line, rubbing his eyes with both hands as he approached. He got down on his knees and whispered a prayer before crossing himself with the Holy Trinity. "I miss ya already, Champ," said Kenny, staring down at the championship belt laid out across his hands. *You made me so proud,* he thought. *You made everybody so proud. Thanks to you, the O'Banion name will never be forgotten. Well done, little brother.*

A tear rolled off Kenny's cheek and splashed onto the belt's golden face. He dried it off on his shirt and stood up. He took a deep breath, wiping the rest of his tears away with his sleeve. "Rest in peace," Kenny cried, tossing Patty's belt down into the grave. Bagpipes began to play again, booming across the cemetery as the championship belt landed gracefully on a bed of long-stemmed roses.

Made in United States
Orlando, FL
17 February 2023

30070232R10200